Habakkuk's Plea

A Prophet of Elohim

Scrolls of the Nevi'im
Book I

S. E. Thomas

Habakkuk's Plea
A Prophet of Elohim
Book I

Scrolls of the Nevi'im

Published by The Dramatic Pen Press, L.L.C.

Lolo, Montana

To
My Loving Husband,
Aaron Michael Thomas,
who brings excitement to our marriage,
laughter to our lives,
and peace to our home.

Table of Contents

Author's Note

Little is known about the real person, Habakkuk. Scholars guess he lived in Judah during the final fall of Jerusalem and the destruction of the Temple of Solomon at the hands of the Babylonians in 586 B.C., perhaps the single most important event in the history of the Jewish people since their release from Egyptian captivity.

The book of Habakkuk in the Bible is only three chapters long, but I have discovered these three short chapters endowed with an incredible wealth of both historical and spiritual insight. While reading them, I found myself greatly admiring this man, Habakkuk, and wishing I could know more about him. After much research, I discovered how little is really known, and I began imagining what his life might have been like. So, I continued with my research and finally wrote this book, hoping and praying all the while that I was in no way misinterpreting God's (Elohim's) message to men or Habakkuk's place in history. So I write this note to my readers so you understand that, while Habakkuk, the kings, and some of the other political and spiritual leaders mentioned herein were real people, most of the other characters are products of my imagination. I have done a great deal of research, however, in order to place them within the correct timeframe, and most of the events I describe in this book are based on historical fact and archeological data.

You may find a great many words, names, and places strange to you, so I have included an extensive section at the back of the book that will explain them for you. It is called "People, Places, and Things." If a character is fictional, I say so there. If, however, I do not label the person as fictional, you may be certain he or she truly lived.

You will also notice that I have opened with a rather long prologue entitled "Hadarah's story." Each of the three books in this trilogy will begin this way—each offering a glimpse into the life of this young girl who lived during the earlier time of the Assyrian occupation of Judah. I included it for a number of reasons, but primarily to provide a cultural and historical background for the time in which Habakkuk lived. You will also find there an intriguing glimpse into one of the main themes of this series—God's promise to preserve a remnant of the Jewish faithful.

I hope you will take the time to read the book of Habakkuk from the Bible and enjoy it as I did, discovering what an incredible person Habakkuk was and what an important message his writings have for us, despite their brevity. And perhaps, this book will help you better understand what kind of life he might have led as well as bring home the depth of his memorable words, "the just shall live by faith."

Blessings,
S. E. Thomas

(NKJV used)

Territory of Ancient of Israel

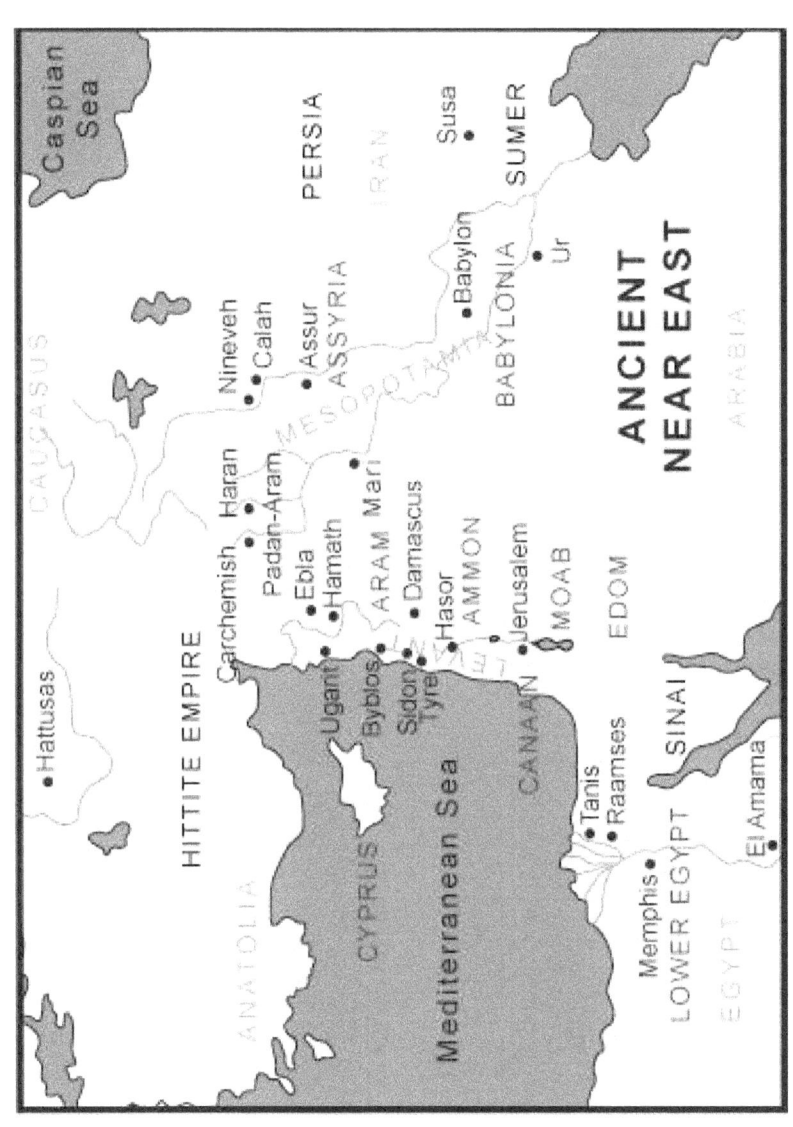

Hadarah's Story: Part I

✡   ✡   ✡

704 B.C.

"The LORD had said to Abram, 'Leave your country, your people and your father's household and go to the land I will show you. I will make you into a great nation and I will bless you; I will make your name great, and you will be a blessing. I will bless those who bless you, and whoever curses you I will curse; and all the peoples on earth will be blessed through you.' So Abram left as the LORD had told him; and—"

Hadarah sighed loudly and rolled her eyes. Her father, Elasah, ceased his recitation of the old story and turned to her, a frown on his face.

"My daughter, you must pay attention. Now you have made me lose my place. Why must I always remind you of this during the recitation?"

"Abba, forgive me… but I do not see how any of those old stories are important."

"Hadarah!" The girl's mother, Dara, chided from her cushion on the floor. "You show your father disrespect! Apologize this instant!"

Elasah raised his hand. "It is all right, my wife. Our daughter is young—only in her eleventh year. I felt the same way when I was her age. She, too, will learn." He turned back to Hadarah. "The stories are our history, Hadarah. They tell us who we are. For who are we, if not Elohim's chosen people? …It is important for you to know how our great God, Elohim, delivered us from slavery at the hands of the Egyptians through his servant, Moses. And how he provided for them in the desert as they—"

"But why would Elohim let the people be enslaved in the first place?" Hadarah asked. "You say He loves us—that He chose us as His special people… but if that is true, why would a loving God allow us to suffer at the hands of such a wicked nation?"

Now Elasah sighed and glanced at his wife.

"She is only repeating what our friends and neighbors say," Dara told him. "Just yesterday, at the well, Hadarah and I overheard the wives of the Lachish city elders talking. They said Elohim abandoned us long ago. This is why they choose to serve the gods of the Canaanites and the Egyptians. They believe those gods will protect us from the Assyrians who crawl our lands and threaten to destroy us as they did Israel."

"I hope you left right away," Elasah said, concern crossing his brow.

"Certainly, we did… as soon as we could."

Elasah gave his wife a blank stare.

"It is very hard to run with full water jugs," Dara added.

Elasah sighed and turned back to his daughter, "Hadarah, we live in very dangerous times; it is true. But this danger has fallen on us because of our unfaithfulness to Elohim. Elohim's prophets even warned us this would happen, but we failed to heed their warning. …Still, no matter what evil may befall us, Elohim promises to preserve for us a remnant of the faithful—for He has a purpose for us that reaches beyond our experiences, beyond this life, beyond what we can see."

Hadarah looked down and played with the hem of her robe, and muttered, "But how can any of that matter to me?"

A month later, Elasah came home with a grin on his face. He pulled his wife aside and they spoke together in hushed tones. Hadarah crept close, hoping to overhear their words. Elasah spotted her and turned. He placed both hands on her shoulders and looked her in the eyes.

"My daughter," he said, a smile on his face. "This day you have been betrothed to Jared ben Reuben. He is a good young man from a good family—one of the few in Lachish who respect the prophets. Soon, we will have a feast to celebrate the betrothal!"

"Jared?" Hadarah asked, her throat tight with excitement, hardly daring to believe her good fortune. Jared, considered one of the most handsome boys in town, had recently been finding excuses to talk to her as she browsed in the *shuk*—the city marketplace—or smile at her as she passed his family home on her way to the well. He was nearly three years her senior. She had not considered him as a possible husband. However, she found that, today, the idea appealed to her. Hadarah looked at her mother. "Imah?" she said. "Is it true?"

Dara nodded, smiling.

"Yes!" Elasah answered for his wife. "Jared's father, Reuben, and I agreed on the bride price only this morning. I was uncertain at first if this would be a good match, but I spoke to the boy and he told me he is considering becoming a rabbi. Hearing this, I knew he would be a good husband for my only child. It will be good to finally have a rabbi of Elohim in town! Within two years or so, you will be married!"

Hadarah's smile faded. *To a rabbi?*

Hadarah leapt across a lethargic rivulet of mud that separated her from her destination, ignoring her mother's voice calling Hadarah's name. In a few short moments she would be outside Jared's home. The rain had finally let up and she felt certain he would be working out in the yard—where he would see her.

By the time she arrived, her hair had curled up in the humidity and framed her face with tiny ringlets. When Jared spotted her, a wide smile spread across his face, but he quickly suppressed it. He was even more handsome than she remembered—but Hadarah determined not to let that dissuade her from her mission.

"Shalom, Hadarah," Jared said, crossing the small yard to lean on the short, mud brick wall separating them. "Why are you out today? Visiting a friend?"

"Uh… yes… a friend," she stammered, afraid to look into his dark eyes lest she lose her resolve. "You, actually."

"Me?" His lip curved up in a playful smile. "I am glad to know I am your friend…. I suppose you have heard that soon we are to become much more."

"Yes. I have heard." She swallowed and nervously swept her long black hair behind her shoulders and straightened her back, hoping to appear more grownup. "I… I have also heard you want to become a… a rabbi."

Jared smirked. "Yes. I find the old stories of our people interesting," he admitted. "It was either that or work in my father's shop all day. As a rabbi in training I would get to travel to Jerusalem to study. I have always wanted to spend some time in Jerusalem. …You could come with me, of course."

Jerusalem? Such an adventure had never occurred to Hadarah. Her friends would be so jealous!

"How long would you… I mean, we, be there?"

"I am not certain. Five years, maybe longer. We would have to return to Lachish eventually, of course, but by then we would have already started our family."

Hadarah blushed a deep red at his last word and looked at her feet. Hearing a nervous chuckle, she dared meet his eyes again and found him also looking away, his ear a bright pink.

"I… I…." she began, trying to dispel the awkwardness, "I think living in Jerusalem would be nice. But I wonder how life would be for us here in Lachish if you were a rabbi of the Hebrew God. He is not much respected here."

Jared met her eyes again, and she saw him shrug.

"I know, but there are far too many priests of Ba'al and Ishtar already. Even the Egyptian gods are overrepresented. As a rabbi of Elohim, I would gain recognition right away. I might even be able to bring peace between the different religions—show the people there is no real difference between us. After all, how different can Elohim be from all the rest of the gods?"

✡ ✡ ✡

701 B.C., Three Years Later

"Hadarah! Get inside now!"

Dara grabbed her daughter and shoved her back as three massive horses came into view, galloping toward them, topped by blood-splattered Assyrian soldiers. Dara tried to block Hadarah from view with her body, but it was too late. The lead soldier spotted the girl and drew his steed to a stop next to the defenseless women.

The Assyrian siege against Lachish had ended. Only this morning, the Assyrian army, led by evil Sennacherib, had completed the mud brick ramp up the outer wall allowing them to breach the city's defenses. The Jewish and Canaanite inhabitants were no match for the swarm of blood-thirsty soldiers. Any of the men who fought back had been slaughtered. Women who too strongly resisted the men's sexual advances had their throats slit. Even now Sennacherib himself oversaw the torture of the city's leadership, as his men worked on setting up a row of impaled bodies along the breached wall—a sign to any who might be considering resisting the might of Assyria. Hadarah had not seen her father all day.

"Look what I found!" the lead Assyrian said, a wicked grin sliding across his face, meeting a jagged scar that marred his left cheek. He slid from his horse, followed by the other two men. "Here," he said to one of them, handing over the reins.

"Master Taklak-ana-Asur," one of the lesser soldiers addressed the battle-scarred man, "which one can I have?"

Taklak-ana-Asur locked his eyes on Hadarah. "Have you ever seen anything so beautiful? …The little one is mine. Do what you will to the mother."

Dara screamed and backed away, trying to keep her daughter behind her. The Assyrian approached, taking his time, knowing the women had nowhere to hide. He reached out and pushed Dara aside. With his left hand, he grabbed Hadarah by the arm.

Hadarah screamed.

Dara attacked the man, trying with all her strength to separate his grip on her daughter.

"Leave her alone! Do not touch her! Leave her—"

She stopped mid-sentence as a club to the side of her head sent her sprawling to the ground.

"Imah!" Hadarah cried in horror. "Imah, no!"

Taklak-ana-Asur grabbed Hadarah around the waist. She kicked, screamed, and struggled, but he easily lifted her on to his horse and climbed up behind her.

"Imah!" she cried, reaching out to her mother. "Imah!"

Dara struggled to lift her head. Blood ran down her face from an ugly gash that exposed her skull. Unable to speak, she reached toward her daughter even as her vision failed. The last thing she saw was an Assyrian soldier galloping away with her screaming daughter slung across his lap.

Habakkuk's Family Tree

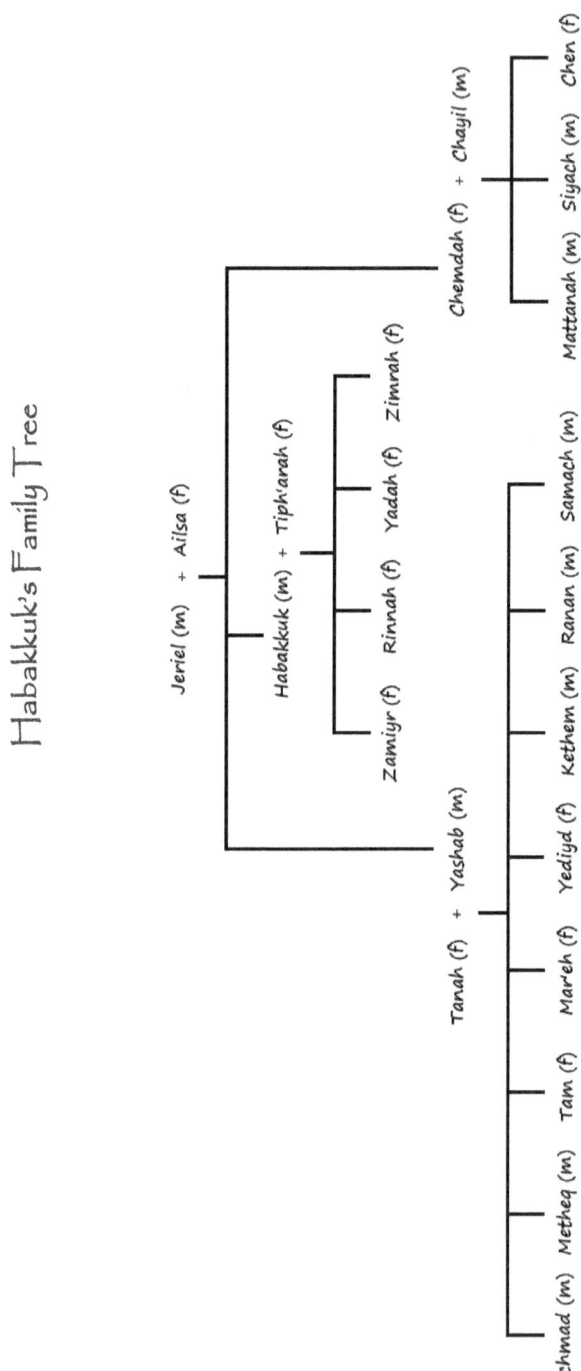

Chapter One: Shachar

✡ ✡ ✡

610 B.C.

Ivah lifted his head and closed his eyes. He grasped the small, stone teraph, carved in the image of his favorite god, and prayed, "Oh, Kothar! Kothar-wa-Khasis! Kothar, Kothar! Kothar-wa-Khasis!"

His voice grew in intensity as he repeated the name. He chanted it again and again for several minutes, getting louder and louder as the Canaanite priestess had taught him. For the gods were wayward, self-interested creatures who had to be coaxed and cajoled into listening to a mere mortal.

"Kothar! Kothar-wa-Khasis, hear my plea!"

As Ivah prayed, he fingered the stone idol of a man holding an axe in one hand and a scroll in the other. He had carved it himself in his free time at the stone quarry he owned. He even paid a local priestess to bless it. Ivah believed his handiwork to be a very clever and skillful rendition and, if this test supplication paid off, he might even consider selling them.

"Kothar-wa-Khasis, the skillful and wise! Oh, master craftsman! Master builder! Maker of weapons, musical instruments, and tools! Oh worker of magic! You who created Ba'al's magical clubs, Yagrush and Ayamur, so he might bring Yam to ruin! It is you I seek this day! Please hear me!"

Ivah waited what he felt was a respectable amount of time and then opened one eye. He saw only the grasses blowing gently beneath the terebinth tree where he knelt. Perhaps the wind was the god stirring. He closed his eyes again, and rubbed the tiny idol more fervently with both thumbs.

"Oh great Kothar! I seek your favor and your blessing! I am a humble man but a good man. I treat my wife well and only visit the temple priestesses for genuinely religious reasons. I have two sons and I have raised them well in discipline and in love of the gods. I have always patterned my life after your example! I work very hard to be like you—skillful and diligent and creative in my work. Please, hear my request!"

Ivah now kissed the stone god and held it above his head.

"I ask only for your blessing, oh great Kothar-wa-Khasis! Increase my holdings! Make me a respected man among my people! Make me prosper!"

Ivah smiled as he made his way back to the worksite. He felt certain his prayer had been heard. For, immediately after his prayer, a small bird had come to perch on a branch in the tree. It had a fat worm pinched in its beak. Surely, that was a good sign.

Today he, his sons, and hired men had been paid to deliver stone blocks to a new worksite and help stack them into position in a new wall. If all went well, this would be the first of many well-paid jobs. Good thing Kothar would be looking out for them today.

"Sakal, how many trips do we have left?" Ivah asked his oldest, a robust man of twenty-three, married and already father to two sons of his own.

"The last one just arrived," Sakal answered, gesturing to a series of stone blocks being unloaded from a sturdy cart hitched to a set of six oxen. "We have begun stacking the last ones along the wall. Everything is going well. I expect we should finish by sundown."

"Wonderful, son! Wonderful! I knew you would have everything under control. How is Shachar doing?"

"Shachar is eager to help, but tends to get in the way," Sakal admitted of his younger brother.

The boy, a handsome lad of thirteen, though legally a man, yet resembled a child in both manner and appearance. However, he meant well and worked as hard as he played. This was his first trip to a worksite, though he had often helped out at the quarry.

"Ah, well, I suppose he will learn in time," Ivah said, waving the matter aside. "How does the master like the work? Has he been by?"

They discussed the project's progress, the cleanup to be done at day's end, and the expected payment. Ivah then turned to inspect the work yard. Only one row of stones remained to be placed along the top of the nearly finished wall. His best worker, Me'ah, having finished up a discussion with the site manager, now headed toward a group of workers, a long scroll in his hand. But Ivah's youngest son, Shachar…. Where was Shachar?

"Oh, no!" Ivah's eyes opened wide. He spotted his youngest son on the top of a scaffold. It looked like he was attempting to move one of the stones by himself. "Sakal! What is your brother doing up there?"

Sakal turned to see his brother fidgeting with the safety cords. "Shachar!" He yelled, breaking into a run. "No! Stop!"

Ivah, too, ran toward the scaffolding. To his horror, Me'ah also headed that way, only the worker seemed completely oblivious to Shachar's presence above. He walked directly under the scaffolding and the massive stone.

The stone teetered. The sound of splintering wood reached them.

"Me'ah! Look out!" Sakal cried, reaching in vain toward his friend as he ran.

Me'ah stopped and looked up just in time to see a massive stone block hurtling toward him.

✡ ✡ ✡

His tongue flicked over fat lips, detecting remaining crumbs and the faint flavor of honeyed wine. Nebelah stood at a distance, watching the so-called prophet. Dirt and sweat gathered on the back of his neck, even though he stood away from the dusty melee of milling, shouting people buying and selling livestock just outside the Sheep Gate of Hebron. His gaze narrowed, following Habakkuk and his large, Egyptian bondsman, Raphad, as they interacted with their customers, stepping over the ropes into the make-shift sheep pens to drag an animal forward, run a hand over its curly, white fleece, and lead the examination of hoofs, limbs, and teeth as the frightened creature bleated protests.

Nebelah sighed and approached from behind, eager to finish this detestable business. But before he could make his presence known, a young man stepped through the crowd and addressed the sun-bronzed, Hebrew prophet. The noises of the sheep market made it impossible to catch the words. Normally, Nebelah would have simply pushed his way to the front of the line. After all, he did not come to buy sheep. But today he had reasons for behaving himself, and the look of the young man intrigued him.

Obviously, the fellow was not from Hebron, but from one of the poor, surrounding villages. His tunic, though stitched securely, was thickly woven and had never been dyed. A patch at his hip and tatters at the hem revealed its age and overuse. His sandals—what remained of them—barely held to his filthy feet. Pieces of brittle leather dragged in the dirt as he walked. He held a small bag, clutched in his right fist—not nearly enough grain or beans for the purchase of even the scrawniest of Habakkuk's lambs. This would be over quickly.

However, a moment later Nebelah watched in surprise as the young man walked away, leading not one but two fat sheep. Nebelah smiled and chuckled, knowing his mission would be successful. He pushed his bulbous frame in front of an elderly man and addressed Habakkuk without ceremony, "Do you always give your sheep away to strangers? How do you clothe and feed your children?"

"Shalom, Nebelah," the prophet sighed the common Hebrew greeting. "Elohim has blessed me so I can, in turn, bless others. And, when that man returns at shearing time, I may actually be ahead in the bargain."

"Shearing is months away! That man will take the sheep and you will never see him again!" He laughed.

Habakkuk glanced at the man and the sheep as they walked away, getting farther and farther down the dusty trail leading away from the city. "You may be right, Nebelah. But Elohim has commanded us to help the needy. I can only obey. I cannot obey for others."

"That man does not believe in your God, Habakkuk. I saw the sign of Ba'al about his neck. He does not believe."

Habakkuk smiled. "Perhaps one day he will."

Nebelah paused. Knowing he needed this man, he rethought his tactics.

"You are a good man, Habakkuk," he began again, "though too generous. I suppose that is forgivable! Some day you will have all the poor in the city sitting at your doorway! But then, who would know? You would be one of them!" He laughed heartily, despite his resolve to tread lightly. Seeing the annoyance in Habakkuk's eyes and detecting the taller man's desire to continue with business, Nebelah cleared his throat and adopted a more serious tone. "But this brings me to a problem the other city elders and I have. A young man came to the city last night while the moon was high in the sky. He came silently and with much fear."

Nebelah saw understanding beginning to show in the prophet's eyes and posture. Another killer had come to Hebron to escape vengeance from the family of his victim.

Hebron, a city of refuge, bore the responsibility of keeping him safe unless the blood-avenger—the closest relative of the deceased man—came to claim him. A trial would then be held and, if it was discovered he committed murder out of malice or purposeful intent, he would be handed over to the kinsman and be at his mercy. If the council determined the death had occurred accidentally, he would be kept safe within the city. However, if he ever left the city—for any reason—and the enemy clan found him, he would be killed. The refugee would only be able to return to his home in safety if and when the current High Priest, Azariah, died. This was unlikely to happen any time soon, though. Azariah, still relatively young, had only taken office last year, upon the death of his father, High Priest Hilkiah.

"The man who came," Nebelah continued, "killed a co-worker by letting a large stone fall on him in a masonry yard. The stone crushed the poor fellow to death. What remained was barely recognizable as a man." Nebelah paused, letting the gruesome imagery play in his listener's mind.

To Nebelah's disappointment, no gasp of horror escaped Habakkuk's lips. No flicker of disgust crossed his brow. He merely waited, saying nothing. This man had the personality of a stone! No wonder the Hebron elders had not invited him to join their circle! Nebelah picked the dirt from under a thick thumbnail and hurried on, "We have not yet held council to decide his guilt or innocence. He is very young, Habakkuk. He is but only in his thirteenth year and no other family in Hebron is willing to take him in— believe me, I have asked." Again he waited for Habakkuk to draw the logical conclusion. But, to Nebelah's deepening annoyance, Habakkuk remained silent.

"He could work in your garden or stables as a slave. You have recently had a man leave you, have you not? Do not tell me you would let him live in the streets—not after giving your sheep away to a stranger!"

Nebelah waited with uncommon patience, feeling the heat of the day intensifying and the places under his arms and beneath the folds of his belly growing moist with perspiration. He kept his eyes on the prophet's face. He heard the sound of Raphad, the oversized, bald Egyptian taking a long swig from a water skin. Nebelah knew the servant's eyes had never left him, but resisted the temptation to notice.

When Habakkuk finally replied, "I will meet him," Nebelah smiled, taking the response as full agreement.

"I knew you would do the right thing, Habakkuk," he said with a confident smile. "His name is," he paused, taking a moment to draw the name from his reluctant memory, "Shachar. He will replace your missing worker. He will be a benefit to your family. Who knows? With his help you might even afford to come back next month to give away more sheep!" Nebelah then burst into laughter, finding himself very funny, indeed.

Nebelah sensed the prophet's reluctance, even as Habakkuk followed him back through the Sheep Gate and down the crowded road, leaving his servant to conclude the business of the day. The man of God had a wife and four daughters at home, whose safety he undoubtedly considered. Other men had fled to Hebron, proclaiming their innocence, only to kill again. But Nebelah cared nothing for Habakkuk's worries. His home had been disrupted enough by the miserable youth and he wanted him out. So, despite his annoyance at having to ask this self-righteous, hard-eyed man for a favor, Nebelah knew his best chance at getting rid of the boy, short of handing the child over to his accusers himself, was to appeal to Habakkuk's overly developed sense of social and religious duty. Nebelah's plan was working splendidly.

After a rather long walk, during which the dispassionate prophet kept falling further and further behind, they arrived at the entrance to Nebelah's luxurious house made of stone. A young, female slave opened the gate and Nebelah led his guest through a rich courtyard, decorated with flower-bedecked shrines and statues in the likenesses of Canaanite gods and goddesses fashioned from stone, clay, and wood. A stone carving of Ba'al stood in the center, standing about half the height of a man and dressed in armor. He held a staff in one hand and a scepter aloft in the other. Opposite him stood Ba'al's consort, the goddess Ashtoreth—a nude, buxom figure of a woman shaped out of clay. Two sets of wings graced her back and she held a serpent in each hand.

Flowers and herbs grew in a lush garden all about the figures and a gingery-sweet scent filled the air. The slave girl ran ahead of them to open the door to the house. She opened it wide for her master.

Nebelah hesitated at the threshold and then leapt quickly inside, making sure not to let his feet touch the threshold itself. Neither did he want his body to linger in that space so that he might not disturb the spirits he believed resided there.

Habakkuk followed. He made sure to step on the threshold itself. With both feet. Nebelah frowned, but said nothing and indicated his new guest.

Habakkuk turned his eyes to a figure on a low bench by the wall. He sat, eyes wide and searching, with one arm wrapped around his front and the other bracing himself against the bench, ready to protect himself or bolt away at any threat. His clothes and face bore smudges of dirt and a large tear marred the hem of his thin tunic. He wore no belt and, therefore, had no silver. His feet were bruised and bare. He had dust-covered black hair, a smooth face, and the skinny frame of a teenager. He looked hungry. Contrary to the Hebrew tradition of hospitality, Nebelah, born of a Canaanite woman, rarely fed these stragglers.

Nebelah approached Shachar. "Boy!" he said roughly. "This man will take you to his home until council is held on your behalf. You will work in his garden or with his sheep or cattle or in any other task he gives you. You will obey him in everything."

"Wait, I—" Habakkuk began.

Nebelah ignored the protest and continued to address the frightened child. "Do you understand what I have said?"

Shachar shrunk back against the wall, wide eyes glancing from one imposing face to the other. He nodded, almost imperceptibly.

"Get up!" Nebelah said to Shachar. He then turned to Habakkuk. "Do not be afraid to whip him if he disobeys. He will learn you are master soon enough. Just use a firm hand."

As Habakkuk and Shachar stepped from the house into the courtyard, Nebelah closed the door firmly after them. Habakkuk blinked in the sun, but the boy kept his eyes on the ground, concentrating on his feet as he followed this large, silent man from Nebelah's opulent home. As the Sheep Gate again came into view, Habakkuk stopped and turned to Shachar.

"My son," Habakkuk said, looking into the boy's eyes. "Do not be afraid. You will not be mistreated in my home. You will have a good job, a warm bed, and enough food. My wife will make you a new tunic and cloak, and my servant will fashion new sandals for your feet. I only ask for your obedience."

Shachar did not look up while Habakkuk spoke, but nodded in understanding. As they started walking again, Habakkuk glanced back to be sure the youth followed. He pretended not to notice the tears tracing dirty paths down the boy's cheek.

Chapter Two: A New Home
✡   ✡   ✡

Raphad glanced up at his master's approach, noting the new addition to their party. As directed, the servant had made preparations to conclude business early. He had refilled their water skins, packed the donkey with bundles of fruit and grain collected as payment, gathered the rope fence into a circle now hanging from one muscular shoulder, and frightened the few remaining sheep into a huddled mass, ready to be driven with sticks back to Habakkuk's home. The heavily muscled, dark-skinned man now stood waiting, eyes watching them as they approached, ready to move at the slightest nod or look from his master.

A glance told Raphad all he needed to know. Soon the sheep bleated their way down the dusty path back toward the city, concerned only with staying away from Raphad's heavy staff. As the party passed back through the Sheep Gate, Habakkuk asked, "Where are you from, Shachar?"

"Lachish," Shachar replied, almost inaudibly.

"Are you of the tribe of Judah, then?"

"Yes, Master."

Habakkuk, a quiet man himself, tried to think of more to say. Nothing came to him for a while, so he finally asked, "Do you have any experience with sheep or cattle or any musical craft?"

"No. My father was a—"

Shachar trailed off and Habakkuk did not press him further. Naturally, his father was a stoneworker or builder. Why else would he be working with large stones? By the look of the boy Habakkuk guessed he had fled Lachish yesterday afternoon or evening. He must have traveled all night long to arrive in the middle of the night at the gates of Hebron, the nearest city of refuge. The uneven road from Lachish cut through rough, hilly country and, though the moon had been full, Shachar's feet, calves, and clothing showed signs of a difficult journey.

Habakkuk's home, built by his own hands five years ago, was a two-room structure made of plaster-covered stone located just inside the southern wall of Hebron. The family room, directly ahead, jutted away from the bedroom at a right angle and an open-air, dirt courtyard occupied the center. Raphad's tent stood opposite the family's sleeping quarters. The front door of the home faced north, toward Jerusalem. A large garden grew to the east side and, to the west, a corral for sheep and cattle shared a wall with their bedroom. Normally it housed only their donkey and the few sheep and lambs needed to provide meals for unexpected guests but, on days like today, it held the sheep they had for sale, offering them very cramped quarters indeed.

The flat, solid roof topping their sturdy home provided both shelter and additional living space, accessed by a simple wooden ladder. A low wall ran around the entire roof, according to Jewish law, to keep people from tumbling over the edge. Eventually, Habakkuk hoped to build a permanent third room where Raphad's tent now stood, but could not yet afford such a project.

As they approached, Habakkuk saw his wife, Tiph'arah, standing in the doorway waiting to welcome him home, as was her custom. How she knew they were coming, he knew not, especially since they returned earlier than usual. Perhaps the noise of bleating sheep alerted her, but it was a common enough sound. Habakkuk had never asked her to wait on him this way, but it warmed him to see his beautiful wife eager for his return. Even after twelve years of marriage, he often found himself entranced by her supple form, flowing, black hair, and large, smiling eyes. Habakkuk firmly believed no woman more beautiful than she could exist. But today, as he neared with Shachar following close behind, concern marked her brow.

"My wife, this is Shachar. He will be living with us for a while. He will take the place of the servant we lost last month. He has had a troubled journey and is hungry."

"Welcome home, Shachar," Tiph'arah said warmly and smiled. "Shall we butcher a lamb, my husband?"

Habakkuk had not planned on this, considering the circumstances, but Tiph'arah managed to hit on the perfect way to welcome the young man using typical, Jewish tradition.

Habakkuk turned to his servant, Raphad. "Raphad, please butcher a lamb for this evening's meal and bring it to my wife." Raphad, showing no surprise, bowed slightly and headed toward the corral. Shachar's eyes widened at this extravagance, but he said nothing. Turning to him, Habakkuk said, "Come. Meet my family."

Habakkuk introduced the silent, dirt-streaked boy to his wife and his four daughters. Normally Zimrah, the youngest at age four, would have eagerly hugged the newcomer and begun an onslaught of cheerful chattering. She was far too outgoing around strangers but, as the baby of the family, Habakkuk and Tiph'arah indulged her. Today, though, she merely took Shachar's hand and led him inside. Somehow—even in her youth—she noticed a difference—a need in his personality that calmed her otherwise boisterous nature.

The older girls smiled politely and then returned to their various chores. Tiph'arah disappeared into the bedroom and then reappeared with Habakkuk's spare tunic. Shachar glanced from her to Habakkuk, afraid to accept it. Tiph'arah took one of Shachar's timid hands in her own and placed the garment into it.

"You can change in the bedroom," she said in quiet but firm tones. "You will also find a jug of water, clean towels, and a vial of oil, so you can wash and be refreshed from your journey. Tomorrow my daughters and I will weave you a new cloak and, when the skin from the lamb dries to leather, you will have new sandals."

Shachar nodded a quick, short bob of the head, unable to look at her, before proceeding to the bedroom.

Tiph'arah raised her eyes to her husband as the boy left. Habakkuk stepped near her and whispered what he knew of the boy. He then adopted a more casual voice and described Nebelah's obnoxious visit and the business of the day. She listened as she prepared a stew of garlic chickpeas to accompany the braised lamb.

Later, Shachar emerged from the bedroom clad in the fresh tunic, his face and hands clean, his hair wet and smelling of cleansing olive oil. He was indeed a very handsome youth, with a smooth face and comely features. His black hair curled up when wet, making him look even younger. Despite the improvement, his shoulders still drooped and his light-brown eyes remained downcast. Habakkuk decided to take him to the roof so they could talk in the cool of the evening without getting in the way of the women as they cooked. Zimrah followed them, not wanting to let the stranger out of her sight.

A large piece of thickly woven cloth, made from flax and stretched over a wooden scaffold created a shady reprieve on the roof of the sturdy home. Habakkuk invited Shachar to sit with him. Zimrah sat at their feet. Only now did the youth allow himself a better look at his new master. Habakkuk was dark-haired, tall, and broad shouldered. Though larger than the average Hebrew, he was not so large as Raphad. His oval face bore rugged, masculine features—high cheekbones, straight nose, bronzed skin. A short, thick, well-groomed beard concealed a good part of his face, drawing attention to wise, gray eyes—eyes that caught details most men missed.

Despite Habakkuk's quiet nature, he bore himself in strength and confidence, both expecting and receiving complete respect and obedience from his servant and family. Though seemingly unbothered by long silences, he spoke with sure words. Shachar could not guess this unusual man's thoughts, but a peacefulness in his new master's demeanor compelled him toward respect and trust.

Habakkuk offered Shachar a drink of wine, which Shachar obediently accepted. After Habakkuk also took a long drink of the sweet liquid, he asked, "Does your family know where you are, Shachar? Is there someone who should receive a message about your safety?"

"My father and mother sent me away after—" he stopped abruptly and began again. "They know I am in Hebron—or at least, they were hoping I would make it here safely."

"Then I will send Raphad tomorrow to Lachish with a message to them of your whereabouts. They will be glad to know you are safe. Is there anyone else?"

"Just a brother, but he and his family live with my parents. There is no one else... and, thank you."

Habakkuk nodded and took another sip of wine, thinking of the enormous tragedy facing, not only this boy and his family, but also the loved ones of the deceased man. As word of this disaster spread, Shachar's family would undoubtedly struggle—losing friends and business connections to the shame it would bring. Habakkuk wondered if the victim had left behind a wife or children. He sighed, finding it difficult to grasp the enormity of the sorrow and loss of the young man before him—barely out of childhood and dealing with pain and shame that could crush a grown man.

They sat in silence for several moments. Zimrah played with some pebbles and a broken piece of pottery at their feet, imagining the pebbles were people and the piece of pottery was a house or tent. She sang a little made-up tune as she played, quite lost in her imagination. Habakkuk usually enjoyed sitting in silence with a friend or family member. It was a comfort—a time when words were not overused or relationships forced. Today, Zimrah's childish noises nicely dispelled what threatened to be an uncomfortable silence.

After a few moments, to Habakkuk's surprise, Shachar initiated further conversation.

"I want to thank you," he began slowly. "I do not deserve to be brought into your home or given a job or borrow fresh clothing," he indicated the tunic he now wore with a pinch of the sleeve. "I promise I will do my best at whatever task you give me. I will try hard to earn.... I will...." he trailed off lamely.

"I am sure you will," Habakkuk assured him. "Tonight we rest. We will eat a good meal together with my family and Raphad. You will sleep in the tent there below with my house servant. In the morning there will be much to do. I recently lost a worker and I have no sons, but I have two other servants tending to the rest of my flock in the valley. However, they are sleeping there tonight and Raphad must go to Lachish, so tomorrow it will be up to me to drive the remaining sheep down to the men so the animals can eat. You must stay here, but there is much work to be done around the house and sheep pen while I am gone. You will have little time for yourself, but...."

"I am glad for that," he said, with near eagerness in his voice. "I would like to be busy."

Habakkuk nodded.

Work would help occupy his troubled mind. It would stave off the depression for a while, but Habakkuk knew of something that would help even more. Did this young man know how to pray? Probably not. Most young people these days—even if they were raised in a Jewish home by parents faithful to Elohim—did not know how to pray. This teaching had been lost completely under the evil reign of King Manasseh. And even though Elohim had given them good King Josiah to help them remember their faith, many towns did not have the local leadership to teach people even the basic principles of Judaism. The traditions had been lost for so long the revival of them was slow. And with the Canaanites, Egyptians, and Assyrians moving into their lands, many had been drawn away by their enticing foreign religions. Most Hebrews seemed to think it acceptable to worship Elohim on Shabbat but keep idols in their homes for protection during the week. The people did not understand how these two beliefs could not—should not—coexist. Even priests, at times, sanctioned this blasphemy. It was difficult to know who believed fully in Elohim and who did not. But there were those who had given themselves fully to the LORD, who had begun practicing traditional Judaism and taught their families the one true Way. Could Shachar possibly be from one of these families? If so, this dark journey would be much easier.

"You should pray, my son," the prophet said bluntly. "Our Great Elohim—the Elohim of Abraham, Isaac, and Jacob—will guide you through this dark time."

"You are right, Master," Shachar agreed. "I have been praying."

Habakkuk was surprised. He waited for Shachar to continue. After a while Shachar added reluctantly, "…but my prayers go no higher than I can reach. Forgive me, but I sometimes wonder if the gods sleep."

Habakkuk swallowed back ire at the mention of the gods.

"The gods of the Canaanites do sleep. They are powerless, faithless, and evil. But Elohim—the Creator of all things—does not sleep. Be assured. If you pray to Him and Him alone, He will hear you. Give Him time to show it."

"Yes, Master, I will."

Of course Shachar had no choice but to give Elohim time. The refugee would be going nowhere.

They sat in silence for a while, listening to the evening sounds begin—loud greetings from neighbors just arriving home or passing one another on the dirt path, sheep bleating as they were led into corrals, cattle's sleepy lowing after a long day of grazing in the sun. From where the men sat they saw the city of Hebron stretching before them to the north, as their house rested at the very southern end. Beyond this lay the now dimming hill country separating them from Jerusalem.

Sprawling vineyards and farms crawled along some of the hills. Others were dotted with cattle or covered in thick forests. To the south, just out of sight, spread vast, rich pasturelands. Even now Habakkuk's shepherds cooked their dinner over a campfire amidst the tall grasses of the Negev. The sheep had, no doubt, already been rounded up into a large area fenced with stones. At night one of the men would lie down to sleep in front of the single, narrow entrance to keep the sheep safe inside while providing a defense against jackals, lions, or thieves. Normally, two or three more shepherds would sleep nearby for added protection. But, now they were short-handed. Unfortunately, Shachar's presence, despite Nebelah's assurances, did nothing to alleviate the problem. He was bound to the city, never able to leave its gates.

Down below, Raphad brought the skinned and gutted lamb to Tiph'arah near the large fire pit in the center of the courtyard. She deftly slid it onto a spit. Once she had it positioned over two iron prongs, she began to turn it over an energetic fire, catching the juices with a clay bowl and then pouring them back over the lamb. Some of the juices escaped and sizzled in the fire. Zamiyr, Habakkuk's oldest daughter, sat inside kneading bread to make flat cakes seasoned with date honey.

Habakkuk looked east and saw Rinnah and Yadah, his two middle daughters, in the garden selecting fruits and vegetables to accompany the meal. The sound of sloshing water told him Raphad was filling a bowl with water from the large clay water jug. It would be used to wash their hands and feet before the meal. The day had grown long and the dust of the roads covered them. It would feel good to be cleansed.

The lamb began to cook and the tantalizing smells drifted upwards. Habakkuk knew it would not be long now, but his stomach did not receive the message. It knotted and growled in anticipation.

✡   ✡   ✡

Evening descended and soon the night would secure its grasp on the small Jewish town. Tiph'arah stood at a basin washing up clay bowls and Yadah, their precocious, dark-eyed seven-year-old, swept the hard packed dirt floor with a straw broom. It was Zimrah's turn to bathe, so she sat unclothed in a tub—a large, shallow copper bowl—near the warm hearth, scooping bowls of water over herself.

Rinnah and Zamiyr had just settled down with their spindles to start spinning wool into thread for a new cloak for Shachar. It was relaxing work and one they enjoyed doing together.

"Do you think he likes it here?" Rinnah asked, letting her eyes dart in the direction of the tent Shachar now shared with Raphad. She was a skinny, bright-eyed nine-year-old with smooth, black hair that had already grown past her lower back. She had a thin face, dark brown eyes like her mother's, and a cute, pointed nose.

"It is hard to tell," Zamiyr answered. Her sharp dark eyes saw everything, but unlike Rinnah, she usually held her tongue. "He does not complain, but his countenance is downcast."

"I do not think he likes it. I think he wants to go home."

"Yes. He probably misses his family."

"Maybe he will like this cloak we are making him and want to stay," Rinnah brightened. "I hope he likes it."

"He will. You are doing a good job. You will soon be an expert spinner and weaver."

Rinnah smiled at the compliment. She had always idolized Zamiyr, a year her senior. Though they did not always get along quite so nicely, Zamiyr's natural maternal instincts usually won out. She had her father's gray eyes and quiet nature and her mother's gentle, compassionate spirit and ability to anticipate the needs and desires of others. At ten she already displayed uncanny beauty—silken, black hair, perfect lips and skin, and well-proportioned feminine features—causing her parents no end of worry.

Rinnah, though a very affectionate girl, had more energy than her older sister. Never content to sit and work at tedious chores, she preferred to go places and do new things. Sometimes she cut corners to make the task go faster only to have to go back later to fix her mistakes. This had gotten her into trouble on more than one occasion. She loved to go into town to the market with her mother where she always found new things to see and smell and do. But Shachar's presence in the home had made this normally tedious chore less bothersome.

Rinnah twined more wool between her thin fingers. "Do you think he is married?"

"I do not think so. His beard has not even come in yet."

"But he could be betrothed."

"Maybe...."

"I think he does not know much about sheep. Did you see the way he walked with them as they came down the road? He was right in the middle of them—right in the middle of the pack—like he did not know they would scatter. Father had to point him to the edge."

"Not everyone owns sheep," Zamiyr replied.

"Do they not have sheep in Lachish?"

"Probably, but if he lived in town he might not have been around them much."

They worked a few moments in silence and then Rinnah whispered, "Do you think he really meant to kill that man?"

"That is enough, girls!" Tiph'arah cut in sharply from where she sat drying a very sleepy Zimrah on her lap. "Less talk, more work! Remember," she said, quoting from the Holy Scriptures, "'a gossip separates close friends'!"

A moment of guilty silence passed and then Rinnah leaned in close to Zamiyr and whispered, "But we do not even know him yet."

Zamiyr shot her sister and hard, disapproving stare and glanced back to see if their mother had heard. Thankfully, she had not.

A little while later, they heard men's voices from outside. At first they could not make out the words, but the final comment they heard clearly.

"I would just as soon hand the murderer over and be through with this whole business!" Nebelah's voice filtered through the open window. "But there is to be a trial for him in five days' time, first thing in the morning. Priest Cheresh will have returned from Jerusalem by then. So, make sure the boy comes. You must to be there, too."

The voices stopped and the front door opened. Habakkuk entered and informed Tiph'arah that the boy would soon be required to stand trial. The blood-avenger had come to claim Shachar.

Chapter Three: The Vision

✡   ✡   ✡

Habakkuk stared intently, but saw nothing in the unusually dark space of his room. Where were the stars? Where was the moon? Some of their light should be shining through the windows. And suddenly, even as he thought these things, light appeared. Only it came not from any window or lamp. Instead, it emanated from the wall opposite him, springing a small point in the stone. He slowly drew himself to a sitting position on his pallet on the floor, never shifting his eyes from the light dripping from the stones like molten lead. As he marveled at this, he saw a small fire burning right out of the middle of one of the rocks.

Does Tiph'arah see this?

He glanced around, but darkness concealed the rest of the room. The light never reached beyond a few handbreadths from the flames. The ring of flames began to grow. It swelled wildly over the rocks in an ever-expanding circle.

I must put it out!

But, though nothing restrained him, he found he could not move. He sat bound to his pallet by invisible cords.

Hungry flames licked the stones. Habakkuk felt the heat on his face but was powerless to stop it. He tried to cry out to warn his sleeping family, but no sound escaped his lips. And now the flaming circle reached from floor to ceiling.

"Get up," came a powerful, trumpet-like voice. The sound surrounded him like thunder, and yet it was gentle to his ears. The words within the voice were deep and commanding. Habakkuk looked in vain for the source.

"Get up," it came again, and Habakkuk found he could move. He obeyed and rose trembling to his feet.

"Step into the fire," came the terrible, bodiless voice again.

"I will be killed," he thought more than spoke.

"Step into the fire." The voice was gentle, yet insistent.

Habakkuk walked toward the angry fire that threatened to consume him. His knees and hands shook, and his breath came in gasps. He lifted his right, bare foot and stepped unsteadily into the flames. The intense heat and pain he expected never came. Instead, he felt cold. A strange, wild wind blew chaotically about his feet and legs.

Habakkuk no longer stood in his bedroom. Neither was he in Hebron. And yet, this hillside looked familiar. Looking north toward the top of the hill, he immediately recognized the holy Temple in Jerusalem built by King Solomon. Looking west, he saw below him the large, impressive palace of the king. A turbulent sky raged above. Flashes of silent lightning passed through the starless expanse—revealing thick, rain-filled clouds. The storm made it impossible to tell what time of night—or day—it was. He realized he still wore only his tunic, cold earth beneath bare feet.

Suddenly, he was not alone. A man passed by him from behind so silently Habakkuk startled. Then, more bodies appeared. The hillside soon resembled a busy day at market with Habakkuk the only one standing still. But, no. The milling people made it difficult to see at first but, as the crowds parted, he noticed a stationary figure, shrouded in black robes, sitting in a heap at the base of a spreading terebinth tree. Habakkuk did not know from where this person had come—nor the origin of the tree. They seemed to have always been there—like a shadow, like uncertainty.

Though Habakkuk did not move from his place, the dark, seated figure and the tree grew rapidly closer—the distance between them shrinking to nothing. He saw clearly now. Wrinkled, withered fingers pulled the black veil from the figure's face, revealing a woman with sunken eyes, gaunt cheekbones, and a toothless mouth. White hair wildly encircled her sallow visage. She bore the look of death—ash gray skin clinging loosely to brittle bones and skull. Only the eyes lived in this wasted corpse.

Habakkuk shrunk from the unclean, old hag. She smelled of decay. The tiny, huddled woman lifted a hand to beg for food. Habakkuk had nothing to give. His only desire was to flee this place. The other people populating the windy hilltop, too, seemed to want nothing to do with her. They passed her by, ignoring the outstretched hand. She called out to them—timidly at first. They did nothing. Habakkuk watched as the hag's demeanor began to change. She stood—weakly at first, but gaining strength. No longer a beggar, she became a huntress. Approaching Habakkuk, the deathly woman shot him a piercing, knowing look and smiled at his confusion. Somehow she knew him.

To Habakkuk's amazement, the hag began to sing—a frail, awkward sound at first. Some of the people glanced her way as they passed. Her voice improved with use. It sifted through the crowd and drew more glances with its purring, enchanting choruses. She was granted nods, and a few even stopped to listen. And as she sang, she began to change.

The hag's lips and cheeks grew fuller, her skin tightened and smoothed, and her hair darkened. The black, tattered robes moved by themselves, swishing and swaying about her body in an unseen wind. Flesh grew on her, filling the emaciated frame to resemble a youthful woman. As she morphed from the hideous to the beautiful, all the while watching Habakkuk, enjoying his fear and wonder. Perfect teeth erupted from toothless gums and the coaxing, seductive smell of honeyed wine and pomegranates replaced the putrid smell which had once emanated from her.

Soon all the people had stopped to gather about her. No longer an old, starving witch, a young, beautiful woman stood before them in gleaming white linen—soft and new and perfect. Her face was young and beautiful and innocent. Lustrous, ebony hair played about naked shoulders, and her sumptuous, womanly form showed alluringly beneath the shimmering, translucent cloth.

This virgin goddess sang in beauty to each person individually, a different melody for each of them—her voice strong, pure, intoxicating. It surrounded them and filled them with longing. It searched them and discovered their secret desires. It whispered to them deep, secret murmurings and made them burn for more.

To the poor she promised riches, revealing ankles and arms laden with golden bracelets, fingers crowded with jeweled rings, and ears dangling with pearls and jade. To the hungry she promised rich food and sweet wine, stepping aside to reveal tables heavy with crisp fruit, soft breads, jars of wine, and roasted lamb and partridge. The enticing aroma wafted around them and made their mouths water. To those desiring power she promised positions of leadership, the acclaim of many, and even the mastery of magical arts. To the lustful she offered her body, silken skin gleaming naked in the light of an increasing storm.

The greedy poor reached for her jewels, but the gold tarnished to clay and the jewels turned to dust in their hands and blew away. The hungry reached for her food but as they brought it to their lips, it grew moldy and crawled with maggots. The power-hungry stepped forward to be blessed, and strength. The lustful reached for her, but cried out in agony as their bodies filled with disease. But still they reached, and ate, and longed.

"What would you have of me?" her sweet, intoxicating voice sang to Habakkuk.

"I will have nothing of you!" he raged.

"Ah, but you will! You will!" Her song turned to a taunting, silvery laugh.

She laughed and laughed, and the crowd continued to worship and desire her. She fattened. As she grew fatter, her worshipers began to starve and sicken. Still they sought her—not with desire, but with desperation. They needed her now. They cried out to her to save them. She laughed as she became fat and oily. The people fell to their knees. Some landed on their faces in the dust. As they crumbled and died, she laughed all the more. Their bodies grew gaunt and wasted and old. Their clothing turned to rags. Their flesh dried up and crumbled from their bones. Her laughter was wild now—hysterical. She looked at Habakkuk and again beckoned.

"No!" he cried.

Even as her insane laughter surrounded him, he could hear her words in his mind.

"Is it peace you seek?" the temptress whispered like a whore. Next to him now, she caressed his face with thick fingers. "I can give you rest. I can bring you peace, luxury, satisfaction. Peace… Peace… Peace…"

And her lies and laughter shrouded him in darkness.

"Peace, my husband," he heard amidst the strange laughing. No. It was not laughter, but crying. And somehow the voice had changed.

"Are you well, my husband?"

He recognized the voice now. It was Tiph'arah. He sat on his pallet, and she knelt beside him. One of her arms encircled him, and the other rubbed his forearm vigorously. He suddenly realized every muscle in his body was tense and trembling. His body felt damp with sweat, despite the cool breeze coming through the window above the place they slept, and he realized he was holding his breath. He released it. It came out ragged and stretched. He coughed and gasped.

"Are you all right? ...Habakkuk?" Fear marked Tiph'arah's voice.

"Y—Yes," he stammered unconvincingly, finally waking from the horror in his mind.

He did not know if he had been awake or asleep. The crying came again. It was Zimrah, also battling a bad dream. He forced himself to breathe in deeply.

"Are you sure? You seemed to be... in another place."

"I am all right," he fumbled for her hand, brought it to his lips, and kissed it. "Thank you. I am fine. Tend to your daughter."

Tiph'arah reluctantly obeyed. Once the child was in her mother's arms, she settled down quickly and her nightmares ended. Habakkuk found no such comfort. Though normal night noises of wind and restless sheep filtered through the window, the vision and laughter continued to haunt him. His mind raced with wonder and his shoulders ached with anxiety until exhaustion finally overtook him a few hours before dawn.

Her eyes—polished ebony—piercing, unblinking, empty. He felt their pressure on his back even before he knew she was there. Habakkuk turned ever so slightly and her gaze met his—an impenetrable stare, both knowing and mindless at once. As he feared, she immediately rose from her huddled position on the ground and came quickly toward him from across the courtyard. He turned away, hoping she might see how busy he was. He had no desire to talk to this woman, and much less be seen talking to her. She was not a welcome sight in Hebron. The people turned away from her when they saw her coming, and those who chose to do business with her, did so in private.

Habakkuk had heard she lived nearby, though not within Hebron. Perhaps she had a shack or a tent in one of the small villages of the Negev. Or, perhaps she lived in an alleyway—he knew not. What he did know disturbed him greatly.

Habakkuk led his donkey toward his usual spot in the shuk, the main city market and gathering place. He arrived later than usual, having remained home longer than usual to prepare Raphad for his journey to Lachish with a message to Shachar's family. The square already hummed with creaking cart wheels, snorting donkeys and the palaver of shoppers and traders. Most of the merchants had already set up their booths and spread their goods and wares out pleasingly.

Today Habakkuk hoped to sell some of his many handcrafted musical instruments—lyres, lutes, harps, timbrels and tambourines, hand drums, flutes, and other varieties of wind instruments. On a few occasions it had been his great joy to see his musical instruments used at Solomon's Temple in Jerusalem to create wonderful music in praise of Elohim. Once he had even made the music himself, joining in with the choruses and harmonies of the sweetest voices he had ever heard. Some of Habakkuk's wooden instruments bore carvings of gazelles, flowers, fruit or other items found in nature. He also hammered simple designs into the metal instruments, where practicality allowed—such as on the bangles of tambourines, but avoided depicting any images associated with foreign deities—such as bulls or lightning. As a man of God by choice and a Levite by birth, he wanted nothing to do with idolatrous practices. But, sometimes, one does not always get what one wants.

The witch approached. Habakkuk turned his back to tether his donkey to a post, pretending not to see her. He untied his largest bundle. But, the woman could not be deterred. She moved as he did to stand so close to his left elbow he could not fail to turn his eyes on her.

"I have what you desire. I have what you search for," she said, dark, unblinking eyes searching his face.

"And what would that be today?" he asked more impatiently than usual, avoiding her stare.

Her rancid breath filled the air and her clothing smelled of smoke and decaying cheese. If her eyes were any less alive they would be lost in the black maze of tattoos covering her face. The wild, symbolic decorations had been designed to frighten evil spirits, but they only succeeded in frightening everyone else. Even the dogs barked and snarled suspiciously at her as she passed, though they never dared come near.

She wore long black robes and a black head covering atop a mass of wild curls. Her hands looked like they belonged to a woman in her sixties, but this woman was probably closer to thirty. Despite the many copper bangles on her headdress, earlobes, wrists and ankles, she moved almost soundlessly. Believed to be a sorceress by many, the townsfolk once threatened to have her stoned. The threats were never carried out, for fear she might call down a curse on them.

"You are a prophet, are you not? I am a prophetess. We are the same, you and I." She waited for a response, but Habakkuk offered none. "You seek answers. I can help you find them. Do you see visions?"

"I do not need what you are selling, woman. If you are hungry, I will share some bread and fruit with you, but then you must go."

Her eyes darted back and forth across his belongings and his person, causing him even more discomfort. He glanced behind to see if anyone witnessed him speaking to her, and pulled a small satchel of food from his pack. He held it out to her. She reached forward to take it but then hesitated and withdrew. She looked suddenly frightened and moved about oddly, shifting her weight rapidly from one foot to the other. Habakkuk could not understand this strange behavior. He opened the satchel and broke off a piece of the bread and ate it. Again, he extended the satchel to her.

"Do you know my name?" she whispered, ignoring his offer and moving close with an intimacy that unnerved him and breath that nauseated him.

Habakkuk knew her name, of course. But, suddenly, Habakkuk knew more than that. He knew her. She was the woman from his vision. He recognized her, despite how the hectic tattoos on her face and hands disguised her features.

"Are you not hungry?" he avoided her question and unsettling eyes.

"My name is Zanah. I am a keeper of sacred items and a priestess of Anath."

Habakkuk knew, as a priestess of Anath, she also prostituted herself. In the Canaanite religion, Ba'al—the great storm god, god of fertility, and king of the pantheon—and Anath, his sister and consort, played significant roles in the cycle of seasons. They told a story that drew their hearers into a world of magic and mystery, love and loss, grief and ecstasy. Ba'al battled his archenemy, Mot, the god of death, and was brutally killed. All nature became unproductive. The crops failed and drought plagued the land for seven years. The god of fertility had died! Then, in a great fury, Anath sought to avenge his death. She hunted down Mot and killed him in a bloody, violent rage. Ba'al then returned to life, mated with Anath, and the drought-stricken land became resplendent with life once again. And so, each fall and winter represented to the Canaanites the duration of Ba'al's death. In the spring, Ba'al came back to life and blessed the ground with fertility throughout the summer and early fall.

According to the priests and priestesses of Ba'al, the ground regained its fertility as Ba'al and Anath annually mated. They taught that Ba'al and Anath desired to see people engaging in this sacred sexuality as a sign of worship. If they performed well enough and often enough, the land would be blessed. The best places, of course, for the gods to receive sacrifices and watch the people performing sexual orgies as ceremonies of worship was high on a hill—as close to the heavens as possible. If a tree, preferably a terebinth, were not already growing on the selected hill, they would build an altar and erect a wooden or stone pillar—a sign of fertility—to bless their rites.

Josiah tore down these high places and desecrated their altars but, though Canaanite priests and priestesses were no longer publically accepted in Judah, they lingered. Generations of intermarrying with surrounding idolatrous peoples had left its mark on Judah. Hebron, like Jerusalem and the other Judean cities, allowed Canaanites positions of influence and power. Though worship of Adonai was the only politically recognized religion, they tolerated private idolatry. Many still burned incense on their rooftops to Anath, Shemesh, or even Mot.

Zanah's presence in and about the city served as a constant reminder of the cost the People had paid for their lack of faithfulness to Elohim. She remained, selling her body, hand-crafted charms, magical potions, and teraphim because a market for her witchcraft remained.

"You are known."

"What?" Habakkuk asked, certain he had misheard.

"She knows you. She would have you."

"Who? What are you talking about?"

"She is very powerful. Make no mistake."

Habakkuk had enough of the woman's cryptic whispers. Her presence drew the looks of the other people in the shuk, making Habakkuk impatient to be rid of her.

"Please. Just take the food," he insisted, shoving the satchel toward her.

This time she took it. But before hurrying away, she gave him one last gaze and said, "My mistress finds favor with few. Anath would have you. Do not spurn her affection, or it will go badly for you, Man With The Hard Eyes."

Chapter Four: Judgment
✿ ✿ ✿

One night remained before Shachar's trial. The family sat together in the main room, eating their evening meal. They tried to speak of normal things to help lighten the mood—how one of their shepherds had killed a jackal to protect the sheep, the sale of a harp as a wedding gift for the priest's daughter, the neighbor's request to borrow some leeks. Despite the delicious food before them and the family's efforts at normalcy, Shachar's appetite evaporated.

A knock sounded at the door and Habakkuk rose. He greeted Raphad and the two men and a woman who followed. Shachar's father, Ivah, though short and balding, had broad, muscular arms, shoulders, and torso. Shachar's mother, Na'veh, though tall for a woman, stooped, making it unclear whether she stood taller than her husband or not. Shachar's older brother, Sakal, entered last. Taller than both his parents, he was light skinned and young, with eyes very much like Shachar's. At their entrance, Shachar rose but made no move to approach them. Tension entered the room with them. They had come for the trial.

Habakkuk offered them a place to stay for the night and for as long as they needed. Tiph'arah made the girls vacate their places at the tablemat and moved to set the space with more food for the guests. As these preparations began, Na'veh went over to Shachar and encircled him in a warm embrace. Her eyes moistened with tears as she held him, and Shachar's face became a mask of pain. Ivah and Sakal then also embraced him, but awkwardly and with less warmth. Ivah then turned and faced Habakkuk, bowing at the waist in a gesture of gratitude.

"Thank you," he said. "Thank you for your generous hospitality toward my son and toward us—all strangers to you. I did not expect—" he stumbled, working around strong emotions. "I did not expect to find such a kind, generous family in Hebron. I am touched to see my son here, eating with your family. You treat him like a guest instead of a criminal." At this his emotions got the better of him. He bit his lower lip and his gaze faltered as he tried to right himself. "Thank you," he finally whispered.

"It is a blessing to have him with us," Habakkuk answered, hoping to ease the man's discomfort. "And he is no criminal. He is just a boy."

Ivah's deep gratitude never left his eyes as Habakkuk motioned for his guests to sit and Tiph'arah placed food before them. They spoke of their deep sorrow over what had happened—not only to their own son, but to the family of the man who died. Though they had traveled all day, they ate little. After dinner, Raphad prepared them a place to sleep on the roof. They retired early and only silent murmurings could be overheard in the stillness of the night.

The next morning, Habakkuk and Raphad joined Shachar and his family as they made their way through town to the main city gates. A large room just off the main gate had been set aside for the purpose of holding the trial. Shachar's story had spread through the city, largely due to Nebelah's loose tongue. A buzz of curiosity and excitement followed Habakkuk and his small entourage as they made their way through the city. Many men and women gathered near the city gates as they approached, falling in line behind them or crowding the streets. Habakkuk led the way, Shachar following directly behind him. Shachar's father, brother, mother, and Raphad followed closely, surrounding him and shielding the young man as best they could from curious stares and rude whisperings.

Twenty-three town elders gathered to hear arguments for and against Shachar. The uneven number, strictly required by law, assured no tie vote. Chairs and benches arranged in a semi-circle pattern, focused attention on whoever addressed the court.

Habakkuk stepped into the room, but upon crossing the threshold, Shachar suddenly stopped. Habakkuk looked back at him to see a face stricken with fear, eyes fixed on a tall, bearded man on the far side of the room. Only his profile was visible. He stood engaged in deep discussion with one of the elders. Zemor, a wealthy vineyard owner, stood with them, interjecting comments from time to time.

"Who is it?" Habakkuk asked.

"It is Caphar. He is the father of Me'ah, the man I killed. And his family is with him."

"Let us approach with confidence," Raphad said in his deep voice, still thick with a rich, purring, Egyptian accent even after more than twelve years in Judah. "We should show them you are not afraid of the truth. They will see you have honor. Honor is your best witness."

Shachar, though far from bold, managed to keep his feet moving, even as the men in the room halted their conversations to stare. Habakkuk and Raphad flanked the young boy, looking more like sentries for their height and broad shoulders.

Nebelah, noticing them, approached. "So you did come," he said. "I was beginning to worry." Raphad snorted like an angry horse. "And you brought your Egyptian dog with you, I see."

"Is everyone here?" Habakkuk asked.

"Yes." Nebelah rolled his tongue across his gums, dislodging the remaining bits of bread still lodged there after his noonday meal. "Sit over there and we will begin." He gestured to a row of rickety wooden benches at the southern end of the room. They took their places as crowds of curious spectators filled all the extra seats, stood along the walls, gathered outside the open door, and sat in the windows to overhear the proceedings. They chattered with excitement.

Habakkuk recognized elders of the city dotting the room, still talking amongst themselves. Two government officials, a Levite, a retired soldier, well-known merchants, and respected farmers had come. Several moments passed as they waited for the trial to begin. At length the elders found their seats and the local, Hebron priest, Cheresh, stepped to the center of the room.

After a brief introduction, he said, "Caphar, your son was killed several days ago by that young man there." He motioned to Shachar, who withered. "No one disputes the truth of this. He is Shachar, son of Ivah of Lachish. He came to Hebron to seek refuge. So, we must determine whether or not this act was willfully done or whether it was an unfortunate accident. What have you to say?"

Priest Cheresh motioned for Caphar to step forward, and the man advanced with long, purposeful strides. "That boy murdered Me'ah!" He shouted the words. "Shachar was new to his father's work camp and my son was a skilled craftsman. Shachar is a bumbling fool with the tools. Everything he touches crumbles into useless bits! He had to know his skill was not sufficient to secure him employment. He deliberately pushed that stone on top of my son! He was jealous of my son's great skill. He may look like an innocent child—but do not be fooled! He is a murderer! Murderer!" At this he looked straight at Shachar with passionate hatred. "You murderer! You took my son from me! I will kill you! I will!" He stood, shaking with rage, pointing a finger directly at Shachar, eyes blazing with hatred.

"Peace, Caphar, peace!" Cheresh said, both hands raised and patting the air. "The young man is entitled to a trial by law. If he is found guilty you will have your revenge. But for now, please save your threats."

Though Caphar did not take his eyes from Shachar, he returned to his seat as bidden. The rest of his family then took their turns delivering testimony. Caphar had another son who was too ill to make the journey to Hebron, so an uncle spoke next and then a male cousin. Family member after family member stood to demand justice for Me'ah's untimely death, genuine pain and sorrow etched deeply in their faces and voices. Many wept. All demanded Shachar's life in restitution. Shachar sat between Habakkuk and Raphad, trembling and weeping with each accusation. The faces of his judges remained flat and unfeeling. After the long string of Me'ah's bitter family, Priest Cheresh stood again.

"All of Me'ah's family has spoken, so next I call Ivah, the stoneworker of Lachish, father of Shachar and employer of Me'ah."

The people at the doors and windows began murmuring amongst themselves in anticipation of this new testimony. They noisily passed information back to those on the outskirts of the crowd who had not heard.

Shachar's shoulders tightened with dread. His father stepped to the front of the room, a great weariness in his face. He seemed old, though he had not yet reached his forty-fifth year. He glanced at Shachar, pain in his eyes. The crowd shushed each other loudly.

"I am a stranger to most of you," he began slowly. "I am Ivah, father of Shachar." At the mention of Shachar's name, his voice cracked. He paused a moment and then continued. "I was in the stone yard when this tragedy occurred. I blame myself. I should never have allowed Shachar to manage that stone on his own. He did not yet have the skill and he could not see around it. I blame myself. He did not know Me'ah was in danger until it was too late. He was helping move the stone along a scaffold to the top of the wall we were building. It slipped off." Ivah took in a ragged breath and continued with new force. "But I know my son! He would not do such a thing on purpose! He is a good boy with a good heart. …He would never—" At this he was unable to continue. Sakal stepped to his father's side and put an arm around his shoulders.

"As you can see," Sakal addressed the crowd, "our family is also broken by this tragedy. We are very sorry for the death of Me'ah. He was a good man—"

"How dare you even speak my son's name?" Caphar's angry shout broke the stillness. "You and your family be cursed! May the gods curse you forever—you, your children, and your children's children!"

"Enough!" Priest Cheresh called. "Caphar, you and your family have had your say."

Sakal's handsome, rugged face bore a look of determination. Nearly ten years separated him and his brother, and he had become a respected worker and businessman in his own right.

"We are sorry for your loss," he returned in a sincere tone. "We are sorry for the pain my brother has caused. However, Me'ah broke a very important rule. One is never to walk beneath a scaffold when there is a stone on it. If he had obeyed this rule, which we all knew well, this would not have happened." Sakal paused and then changed his approach. "Few of you know Shachar as I do. He is a tenderhearted youngster and is not capable of willfully hurting anyone. He even cares for helpless and hurt animals he finds, feeding them and mending their wounds. Would a man who cares for sick beasts be capable of intentionally causing harm to a man? He is a compassionate young boy.

"And, yes," he continued. "Me'ah was a skilled worker and a good man, but Shachar was never jealous of him. They were friends! Me'ah often took time to help Shachar learn a new skill and even shared his meals with him. Me'ah's tragic death is a deep wound—not only to his own family, but to ours as well! I entreat you," Sakal turned toward the priest and town elders, "let Shachar stay here in Hebron and live in peace. Do not turn him over to these men who, out of their grief, seek revenge rather than justice. Do not add to the tragedy of Me'ah's death by taking another life. Shachar is very young, but he will learn and grow. He will work hard and be a credit to your city. Please do not allow another family to needlessly lose a son."

Sakal bowed respectfully to the elders, as did Ivah, and they both walked back to their places by Shachar.

Cheresh again stood and shuffled to the center of the room. "Now I will allow Shachar to speak in his own defense." He gestured for Shachar to step forward.

Shachar shrank back.

"Speak," Habakkuk whispered. "You must."

Somehow Shachar found the courage to step forward. He looked around at the many pairs of eyes and wilted.

"Speak your peace," Cheresh ordered mercilessly. "Speak or take your seat."

"I… I want to say," Shachar began feebly, "I am sorry. I am sorry for what I did. I am sorry for not being more careful. I am sorry about Me'ah. He was my friend. It was an accident, but the worst kind of accident I can imagine. I lost my friend, my home, and my family. If you choose to give my life over to Me'ah's family, I would not blame you. I—" Unable to continue, he turned abruptly and returned to his place between his parents.

"Habakkuk," Cheresh called, not willing to rise from his seat. "What do you have to say about this matter? If Shachar is proclaimed innocent, are you willing to offer him a permanent residence or employment?"

Habakkuk rose and faced the twenty-three elders. "I am," he said in a soft, deep, but resolute voice.

"Very well, fellow elders, you have heard the testimonies of all concerned. Let us make a decision quickly—so the travelers can find food and lodgings."

The elders asked everyone leave the room so they could discuss and take a vote. It was difficult to get through the gathered crowd to fresh air, but Habakkuk found a place a street away for them to sit. Shachar's family, however, stood or paced nervously as they waited. Many moments passed. Even the crowd became impatient to hear the final judgment. They meandered about, gossiping and complaining about the work they were missing. Habakkuk found them irritating. Why did they not just go about their business instead of waste time looking for fodder for gossip?

When the elders finally emerged, the crowd, in their eagerness to hear the judgment, prevented Shachar's and Caphar's families from entering the room until two guards came to force them to make space.

"We have come to a decision," Cheresh stated importantly. "Shachar, come to the front, please."

Shachar left his parents and joined Cheresh before his judges.

"We have decided you are to be provided refuge in Hebron." At this, a great sigh escaped the lips of Shachar's parents and brother. Caphar's family, however, became enraged and shouted their protests. Many moments of confusion reigned before order was restored.

"Shachar," Cheresh began again, taking advantage of the tenuous silence. "You must understand what your refuge here in Hebron requires. As long as you stay within Hebron's city walls, your life is your own. You may go peacefully throughout the city and conduct your business. You may work and live as others do. However, you are never—not as long as the High Priest lives—to leave Hebron. If you leave the protection of the city—if you pass beyond the city walls, you put your life in danger. If any of Caphar's family finds you outside Hebron, you will be at their mercy. And, from what I have just witnessed, it is doubtful they will offer you any. They would have the right to kill you. However, if by some chance, High Priest Azariah in Jerusalem dies, all things will be renewed. You would then be free to live wherever you choose. Their legal claim on your life ends with his death. Now," he nodded toward Habakkuk and Shachar's family. "Go back to the house of the prophet in peace, but remember my words."

After a brief invocation, the trial ended. Shachar found his way into his mother's arms. His family spent the rest of the day visiting together at Habakkuk's home. They were quiet about the house—except in their frequent thanking of Habakkuk and Tiph'arah for their generosity. Na'veh, Shachar's mother, took a deep liking to Tiph'arah, her keen mother's eye having noticed the new clothes Shachar wore. The guests then retired to bed early, weary from travel and sorrow, but Habakkuk and Tiph'arah talked for several hours before joining their sleeping children. Once in the sleeping quarters, Habakkuk motioned for her to join him on his pallet. He whispered a prayer for both of the broken families that had touched their lives. Then they lay in each other's arms, allowing silence and sleep to comfort their spirits.

✡ ✡ ✡

Morning noises roused Habakkuk from his slumber and he realized Tiph'arah no longer lay in his arms. The city trumpets sounded in the distance to welcome the morning. The scrapes and clatter of Tiph'arah preparing the morning meal came from the next room. Zamiyr had also risen, but the other three girls yet slept on their pallets nearby. Habakkuk stood and rubbed drowsiness from his face. He walked to a water basin in the corner and splashed some of the cool liquid on his face, washing away the remainder of his lethargy. As he left the room he noticed Rinnah watching him and smiling sleepily. She was spoiled, he knew, and would stay in bed all day if allowed. He gently kicked her feet with his bare one.

"You need to get up," he chided gently, but left her there and went into the family room to greet his wife.

Walking up behind Tiph'arah, he encircled her in an embrace and kissed the top of her head. She smiled, but continued kneading her extra-large batch of dough. The sound of scuffling on the roof told them Shachar's family would soon be down to eat and prepare for their journey home.

Habakkuk went outside and found Raphad between trips. The taller man stood filling the large family-use clay basins with fresh water from the common well, which he fetched two smaller jugs at a time.

"Good morning," Habakkuk greeted him.

Raphad nodded respectfully. It was not his custom to use many words, especially so early in the morning. But despite his silent ways, Habakkuk had known Raphad almost as long as he had known his wife and trusted him completely.

Normally Habakkuk would go to the roof to say his morning prayers, but since they had company he was at a bit of a loss to know where to find privacy. He looked around trying to decide, when Raphad caught his eye and pointed with his chin to his tent. Habakkuk nodded in thanks and reverently opened the tent flaps. He stepped into the simply furnished quarters and knelt on the rug. Though Raphad had lived with them for nearly ten years, Habakkuk rarely entered his servant's tent and never without an invitation. This was Raphad's sacred, private place. Inside lay a bed pallet, rolled up and put aside, the blankets carefully folded and stacked nearby. A wooden shelf contained a folded, spare tunic, a vial of oil, and an Egyptian, carved box made of wood, inlaid with ivory.

In one corner sat a basket containing tools—an iron knife, some odd pieces of flint, a neatly rolled length of rope, and a bundle tied with a cord. Against another wall sat a roughly triangular shaped package, wrapped carefully in a piece of linen. Habakkuk immediately knew what it contained. It could be no other than the lute he had given Raphad a few years ago. Raphad still had not mastered the instrument, but they sometimes heard a gentle plucking coming from his tent in the evenings.

Habakkuk smiled as he thought of this. Though so capable in everything else, Raphad's lack of musical skill presented a bit of a quandary. Too embarrassed to ask Habakkuk to show him how to play until he learned the basics, learning them without instruction proved harder still.

Habakkuk said his ritual prayers, thanked Elohim for his family and his health and then prayed especially for Shachar, Shachar's family, and the family of Me'ah. Even as he prayed for them, he heard Shachar's parents and brother coming down the ladder and being greeted by Tiph'arah. When he finished, he stepped from the tent into the new sunshine, carefully closing the flap behind him. Raphad was nowhere in sight, so Habakkuk headed inside and greeted Ivah, Shachar's father. The man bowed deeply.

"Thank you," he said with such fervor Habakkuk felt embarrassed. But Ivah continued, "You have brought us hope. You and your family are too generous! We do not deserve your kindness."

"Please," Habakkuk answered uncomfortably. "Come. Sit and eat with us. My wife has prepared a meal."

Tiph'arah led them to their places and Habakkuk offered up a prayer.

"I heard you are a prophet," Ivah began, refreshed from his night of rest.

"Yes," Habakkuk responded with a polite nod. "Yes, I trained as a prophet in Jerusalem and I serve the people of Hebron."

"They say you are very wise. They told me about how you warned the people of last year's drought. Is this true?"

"Adonai was gracious enough to show me."

"Tell, me, what do you see of Shachar's future?"

Habakkuk often received these kinds of requests. People were used to going to witches and diviners to ask for prophetic readings. These false prophets would kill a goat and 'read' the entrails or divine readings from bones cast upon the ground. The people did not understand that a true prophet only heard what Elohim wanted him to hear. He could not charm information out of the LORD.

Habakkuk glanced at Shachar and said, "The LORD El Shaddai has not chosen to share that information with me."

Ivah looked disappointed, but pressed him no further.

"It is so good to find such kindness here in your home," Ivah said. "I can only imagine how much business I will lose. We may not even be able to remain in Lachish. There is no one in the city nor even in the surrounding villages who has not heard of Me'ah's death by now."

Habakkuk glanced at Shachar. The boy had stopped eating, but stared intently at his bowl.

"Me'ah's cousin and brother attacked Sakal," Ivah continued, speaking around a mouthful of bread and lentils, "by the city gates just as we were leaving to come here for the trial. Sakal defended himself well. He is strong. But they are very bold… very bold indeed." He took another bite. "My wife gets no sleep from the worry of it."

Shachar sunk lower, his hands in his lap now, looking at no one.

"They did not really attack me," Sakal said, waving the incident away with a gesture. "They simply became angry. Words were spoken. Nothing more."

"But the brother had a stick!" Ivah insisted, looking at Habakkuk rather than either of his sons.

"A walking staff, Abba," Sakal said.

"Their mother suffers as well," Ivah said, chewing furiously. "The other women no longer speak to her. She—"

Tiph'arah rose abruptly, her motion disrupting her bowl and bringing Ivah's long complaint to an abrupt end.

"Shachar, my dear," she said, turning to the boy. "Could you please fetch that jug and fill it with water? We will need it to clean the dishes later."

Shachar rose, took the jug, and swiftly left the room.

When Tiph'arah sat again, Na'veh slipped a hand into hers. Ivah noticed nothing and continued talking about the many hardships his son had caused.

"We should be going," Ivah finally said, standing. He bowed repeatedly as he spoke. "Thank you again for your generosity. We appreciate the wonderful food your wife prepared for us. It will make our journey easy." It was then he noticed Shachar had never returned from filling the water jug. "Where is my youngest?"

"He is outside, Abba," Sakal answered.

They found Shachar standing near the large water jugs. The smaller jar, now full, sat his feet. Hands on the rim of the larger jar, the boy stared into the water at his distorted reflection, but straightened when he heard them approach.

"My son," Ivah said, putting one hand on Shachar's shoulder. "Obey the good prophet. Do as he says and be an obedient servant. He will give you a good life."

"Yes, father."

Na'veh gave him a long, loving embrace and slipped him a small bundle of personal items from home. Ivah turned to Habakkuk, "Thank you also for sending your servant to us. He brought us great relief."

"You are welcome," Habakkuk responded.

Tiph'arah handed Na'veh a satchel of food for their journey, which she accepted graciously. Sakal embraced and kissed his younger brother.

When the family finally headed down the road toward the city gates, Habakkuk felt ashamed at his relief. The prophet obediently fulfilled the Jewish tradition of hospitality but, as a private man by nature, he always felt glad when visitors left. Today his relief at Ivah's departure was more intense than usual. He found the man's profuse obeisance and constant whining annoying. But the family's departure effected Shachar differently. He went immediately to the roof to begin cleaning up after them. He worked hard and ate nothing for the remainder of the day.

Chapter Five: Shabbat

✡   ✡   ✡

Shachar had now been with them four days. The livestock belonging to Jewish people remained penned throughout Shabbat, which began in a few hours, at dusk. Tiph'arah had taken Rinnah and Yadah with her to a field just outside the city gates to gather bundles of grasses to stock the corrals so the animals would have food during the day of rest. Habakkuk met them there, packed the grasses high on his donkey and then journeyed to the pastures to help the shepherds bring the sheep and cattle up to the corrals. Instead of coming home right away, Tiph'arah decided to take her daughters to visit a friend who lived in a small settlement outside the city walls, so Zamiyr and Shachar were left to look after Zimrah. Raphad worked nearby cleaning the stalls.

Shachar and Zamiyr were just about to take Zimrah to the roof to hear a story, when they heard a man's piercing cry coming from the stables. They ran to see what had happened. Shachar entered first to find Raphad doubled over, holding tight to his right thigh. Bright red blood seeped through his tunic beneath his fingers.

"What happened?" Shachar asked.

"I cut myself on a piece of wood sticking out from the wall," he responded through a jaw clenched in pain. "I think I need help."

"I will get Tiph'arah!" Shachar said and quickly turned to go.

"No!" Raphad called him back. "You cannot leave the city!" He gasped and tried to hobble toward them. Zamiyr now stood in the entrance looking in horror at Raphad. "Zamiyr can go."

Zamiyr took one frightened look at him and fled from the stables. She ran into the street as if wolves chased her. Indeed, the fright at seeing the enormous Raphad—who had always seemed impervious to pain—weak with it, gave her new speed. The very fact he had asked for help—something she had never before heard him do—proved he desperately needed it. As she ran, her heart thudded within her chest—not from exertion, but from raw, naked fear.

"Help me get to my tent," Raphad said.

Shachar immediately obeyed and tried to support the enormous man as best he could. They hobbled haltingly from the stables, around the house and across the courtyard.

"Would it not be better in the house?"

"I do not want to get blood on the floor... but, perhaps I should stay in the courtyard where it will be easier for Tiph'arah to help me."

Raphad leaned against the wall while Shachar dragged a small bench to him. The large servant eased himself onto it, his face contorting in a painful grimace.

"You are still bleeding badly," Shachar said, seeing how the blood made a larger and larger stain on Raphad's tunic.

"She will be here soon," Raphad said, his voice thick and groggy.

Shachar went to the front gate and looked anxiously down the road. Tiph'arah was nowhere in sight. They would not be back in time. He had to do something! He ran back past Raphad and into the house. He went to the loom and found a long piece of cord and a small piece of linen.

"Move your hand," he ordered the sleepy giant upon returning. Raphad obeyed and blood gushed. Shachar lifted the tunic from the wound. The gash was deep and a quick stream of bright red blood gushed from it. He quickly applied the linen cloth and tied it tightly over the wound with the cord. Raphad winced in pain. The linen bandage quickly turned red. Shachar pressed down on the bandage as hard as he could. He pressed until his muscles ached and Raphad groaned.

After what seemed like an eternity, Shachar turned to see Tiph'arah running down the road and enter the open front gate. Great relief showed in his face.

"I am here," she called breathlessly. "Do not move! Keep your hand on the wound." She checked the white edges of the cloth. Her eyes betrayed deep concern as she observed how quickly white became red. "Keep pressing. Do not move until I tell you."

Shachar obeyed but watched her as she went quickly to the fire and stirred it up. Then she disappeared inside the house for a moment, only to appear with an iron tent stake in her hand and a cloth. She returned to the fire and wiped the tent stake clean with the cloth before shoving the pointed end into the hot coals. While they waited for the tent stake to heat, Tiph'arah went back inside and returned with a wineskin. She carefully held it to Raphad's lips and encouraged him to drink. He managed to gulp down some of the medicinal liquid. As he drank she spoke gently to him as she might speak to a sick child, even though he was easily twice her size.

Raphad drank what he could but then closed his eyes and put his head back against the stone wall. Shachar's arms ached but he continued pressing. After a while Raphad seemed to be napping. The bleeding had slowed considerably, but still the wound seeped.

Tiph'arah returned to the fire and gingerly wrapped the end of the tent stake with the cloth so as not to burn herself. She took the smoking metal stake from the fire and said to Shachar, "All right. Now. Move the cloth. And hold his leg."

Shachar obeyed and as he did so, a new current of blood began to flow. Shachar grabbed Raphad at the knee to try to steady him for the coming blow. Then Tiph'arah pressed hot end of the metal stake into the open wound where it sizzled and steamed and sent up the smell of burning flesh. Raphad awoke immediately and cried out in a deep wail of pain. His arms flailed back against the wall to steady himself against the blast. The muscles in his leg tightened and his entire body strained, but he managed to keep his leg still.

Tiph'arah removed the stake, leaving Raphad whimpering and breathing deep, ragged breaths. She checked the wound again and then sighed a great sigh of relief. "Praise Elohim!" she said. "The bleeding has stopped."

Raphad again slipped back into a dreamlike state, his breaths deep and ragged. Tiph'arah washed his leg with a damp cloth. Several moments passed as she and Shachar watched him, listened to his breathing and felt for a pulse.

"I think he will be all right now," Tiph'arah said. "We will need to make sure he eats a good meal tonight."

They looked up at the sound of movement at the gate. They saw Zamiyr returning with Rinnah and Yadah. When Shachar saw them he suddenly experienced a terrible sinking feeling. "Oh, no! Where is Zimrah? She was by the ladder when we left her to help Raphad!"

Everyone but the injured servant began an immediate search for the missing four-year-old. Tiph'arah ran inside and Yadah and Zamiyr searched the premises. But soon Rinnah called from the roof. "She is fine! Do you hear? She is all right! Do not fear! She is on the roof playing! I will bring her down!"

Everyone breathed a sigh of relief and their focus again returned to Raphad.

"Should I go fetch father?" Zamiyr asked.

Tiph'arah hesitated. Having Habakkuk there would be a great relief, but Zamiyr had never gone to the distant pastures by herself.

"No," she answered after looking at the sky. "Your father is probably on his way back even now. And the bleeding has stopped. We will wait for him."

By the time Habakkuk returned, Raphad's condition had improved. He had awakened enough to eat the food and drink Tiph'arah brought him. Habakkuk's brow furrowed with worry upon seeing Raphad sitting against the wall with a bloody bandage on his thigh and looking pale while his wife hovered over him. But Raphad gave him a weary, reassuring smile. Habakkuk, the only one in the family strong enough to heft Raphad's considerable weight, helped his servant to his tent so he could rest.

"He sleeps," Habakkuk said with a mixture of relief and concern, sitting down to dinner with his family. "We should check on him in the night, though. He lost much blood and is weak."

He offered up an unusually long prayer, centering primarily on Raphad. Then he spent several moments thanking Elohim that Shachar had been there to save Raphad's life. Habakkuk opened his eyes to find a questioning look on Shachar's face.

"Thank you, Shachar," Habakkuk said to him. "If you had not done what you did, Raphad would not have survived."

"Your wife cauterized the wound," Shachar answered.

Habakkuk looked at Tiph'arah and smiled. He reached for her hand and she slipped it into his.

"She is an amazing woman," he agreed. He rubbed her hand softly with his thumb as he held it. "We are all in good hands, I know." But then he looked back at Shachar. "But I want you to know my gratitude for what you have done." He glanced back at his wife and gave her hand a little squeeze before releasing it. Then he looked again at Shachar. "You acted quickly to slow the bleeding. If you had not, Raphad would have bled to death before Zamiyr had a chance to fetch her mother. You saved his life—the three of you did."

He looked from one to the other and then his gaze settled on Shachar again. He wanted so badly to help this young man realize he had worth—that Elohim had made him for a purpose and had even brought him to be in this very home for a reason—no matter the horrible circumstances. For, though Elohim had not brought evil into the world, He often worked through it and in spite of it to fulfill His good purposes.

Habakkuk then stood. Perhaps the best way to show the boy his worth was to let Elohim tell him. He went into the bedroom and walked to a shelf built into the western stone wall. Retrieving a small bundle, he returned and sat cross-legged on the floor where the women waited expectantly. Habakkuk held the package carefully in one hand while he gently and ceremoniously unwrapped it. The women looked on reverently as they waited for a glimpse of the most costly item they owned. Habakkuk held in his hands a small scroll. It was made simply of tanned leather wrapped around wooden rods, and yet Habakkuk had saved for four years in order to be able to afford to pay a scribe at the Temple in Jerusalem to copy it for him from the Temple scrolls. The scroll contained a section of the Talmud. Habakkuk unrolled it and read from it in soft tones, relishing the choice words of El Shaddai on his tongue. Habakkuk's deep and rich voice read each syllable—slowly, deliberately—letting their meaning have time to sink into the minds and hearts of his listeners.

The scroll told the story of Elohim's deliverance of their ancestors from the hands of the Egyptian armies when they came to the Sea of Reeds. Elohim told Moses to stretch out his staff. Moses obeyed. A strong eastern wind blew and parted the waters. The People crossed over on dry land and, when the Egyptians followed, the sea returned to its place, drowning them all.

"This story speaks of Elohim's power, greatness, and profound love for us," Habakkuk said when he finished reading. "Even though we were mere slaves, Elohim reached out His hand to protect us. We are Elohim's chosen people. We are His children and His heirs. Let us never forget how He has shown us His glory. Let us never forget how He cares for us and will deliver us from our enemies if we call on Him. And let us never forget that our worth lies in Elohim, our Creator. He loves each of us and even though terrible things happen in this world, His love endures."

Habakkuk wrapped the scroll again carefully in the clean linen and returned it to its place. When he returned, they shared a warm meal of lentil stew and rye bread, using the bread to sop up the thick, flavorful liquid. Afterward, they enjoyed figs from their own tree. After the meal, the family did not hurry off as usual to tend to chores. They sat and talked and laughed together at Rinnah's jokes and Zimrah's antics. Shachar waited, unsure of what they expected of him.

"Perhaps I will go check on Raphad," he said and began to rise.

Habakkuk put a hand on his shoulder. "Wait a moment," he said. "My wife can check on him. Sit with us a while."

Shachar remained and listened curiously to their family banter. Tiph'arah returned quickly from checking on Raphad. She reported that he slept soundly. Then, as the sun descended on the horizon, she lit three oil lamps to help welcome Shabbat. The soft light filled the room making the coming of night seem closer and sweeter. Zamiyr pulled the supper mat out of the way. Zimrah still chewed on a crust of bread—being more prone to daydream than finish her meal.

Habakkuk then called each of his daughters to him, starting with the oldest. They came and knelt in front of him one by one. "Zamiyr," he said and placed a hand on her head. "May Elohim make you like Sarah, Rebecca, Rachel, and Leah." Then he kissed her softly on the forehead. In this way he blessed each of the four girls. When it was Zimrah's turn he had to make her put down her bread so she would pay attention. When he was finished, she grabbed his large hand as it rested on her head and grinned up into his face. He could not help but smile at the little rascal. When he finished, she jumped up eagerly and kissed his cheek. He took her small face between his hands and kissed her forehead as he had kissed the others. She giggled. Then Habakkuk turned to Shachar, who had been watching all of these things with a sort of wonder.

"Come," Habakkuk said to him. "Let me bless you as well."

Shachar shyly and awkwardly knelt before Habakkuk as the girls had, though taller than they. Habakkuk placed a hand on his head and said, "May Elohim make you like Ephraim and Manasseh, the two sons of Joseph."

The meal and small ceremony concluded, Habakkuk rose and again retrieved the scroll from the shelf. He took one of the lighted oil lamps and walked out the door into the gathering darkness. Tiph'arah followed him with a bowl of stew topped with a piece of bread on top and a small flask of wine. She returned shortly to see a questioning look on Shachar's face. She explained, "Raphad has awakened and his appetite is good. My husband will sit with him and read to him also from the Torah. Raphad enjoys it so. He would be disappointed to have missed it."

✡   ✡   ✡

The next morning Habakkuk awoke to a brushing noise coming from the roof. He rose from his pallet and noticed Tiph'arah and Zimrah's places already empty. But, walking into the family room, he did not find them there. Perhaps they were on the roof with Shachar making the noise he had heard. He climbed the ladder. What he found horrified him.

"Stop! What are you doing?"

Shachar immediately turned from his sweeping and looked at him guiltily. "I am sorry," he said. "Did I wake you?"

"That is not the problem," Habakkuk answered as he climbed up the rest of the way and stood on the roof. He walked over to Shachar and took the leafy branch from him, with which the boy had been sweeping the dust and leaves from the roof. "It is Shabbat—the day of rest."

"Oh!" Shachar said, immediately ashamed. "Forgive me, Master. I forgot."

"Are you not accustomed to observing Shabbat?"

"Forgive me... no... I know it should be observed, but my father... I mean... there was always so much work to be done—."

Habakkuk's annoyance dissipated as he watched this well-meaning boy stammering before him. "It is all right," he sighed. He put down the branch. "You did not know any better. So many have forgotten to observe Elohim's Shabbat. But in this house it is taken very seriously. ...Do you remember the story I read last night about how our ancestors were protected when their former slave masters pursued them?"

Shachar nodded.

"A slave has no choice but to work. If their masters make them work every single day, they must do it. But we were freed from our masters so we could follow Elohim. We choose to honor Him and His love for us by resting on the seventh day—to remember. We work hard every other day of the week, but we do no work on this day. This day belongs to Adonai."

Shachar kept his eyes cast down as Habakkuk spoke.

"Do not worry," Habakkuk said and patted him on the back. "Look at me, Shachar. It may take some time for you to become accustomed to our ways. But take this day as a gift from Elohim. It is a chance for you to rest and enjoy the gifts He has given you. It is a day for family, for friends, and most importantly, for worship. Come. I will show you something."

Shachar obediently followed the broad-shouldered man back down the ladder.

"I am going to find you a more permanent place to stay," Habakkuk commented as they left the roof. "You cannot sleep under the sky when the rains come. You will need a tent of your own."

They went inside and Habakkuk led him to the corner of the room where his many instruments lay neatly stacked or wrapped in bundles. As he looked through the pile, Tiph'arah and Zimrah entered the room from outdoors.

"Ah," Habakkuk looked up. "Where were you?"

"Zimrah and I went on a little morning stroll so her noises would not wake the rest of you. I looked in on Raphad again. He sleeps peacefully."

"That is good. Rest will help him regain his strength."

"When he wakes I will change his bandage and treat the wound with wine, honey, and herbs."

"Yes… And we must continue to pray against infection."

"Certainly, my husband."

Tiph'arah sat down with Zimrah and used a bone comb on the child's wild hair. Zimrah sang a made up song about birds and berries—possibly stemming from observations on her walk. Habakkuk found what he was looking for amongst the packages. He pulled out a finely made lyre. He turned back to Shachar.

"I have been thinking about what you should do. Now that you live with us, you should put your hands to something useful—not today, of course, but soon I will teach you to play this instrument and then I will teach you how to make them. You can join me in the market and help me sell them."

"I would be honored to learn from you, Master," Shachar said and nodded.

His exceeding politeness reminded Habakkuk of Ivah, Shachar's father. But somehow it was less annoying coming from the boy. Habakkuk smiled.

"Come," he said and they sat on the floor together. Zimrah climbed out of her mother's lap and jumped into Habakkuk's. He laughed and awkwardly reached around her to pluck at the strings. The music rose haltingly from the instrument at first—especially when Zimrah was given a turn to pluck a cord or two. The other girls rose sleepily from their beds, called by the music, and joined them.

"What one should do on Shabbat," Habakkuk said, "is sing praises to Elohim, spend time talking and listening to Him, and enjoy the people He has brought into your life."

With that he lifted his rich voice and sang,

O LORD, *our Adonai,*
How excellent is Your name in all the earth,
who have set Your glory above the heavens!

Out of the mouth of babes and nursing infants
You have ordained strength,
because of Your enemies,
that You may silence the enemy and the avenger.

When I consider Your heavens,
the work of Your fingers,
the moon and the stars, which You have ordained,
what is man that You are mindful of him,
and the son of man that You visit him?

For You have made him a little lower than the angels,
and You have crowned him with glory and honor.
You have made him to have dominion over the works of Your hands;
You have put all things under his feet,
all sheep and oxen— Even the beasts of the field,
the birds of the air, And the fish of the sea
that pass through the paths of the seas.

O LORD, *our Adonai,*
How excellent is Your name in all the earth!

Chapter Six: The Void

✡ ✡ ✡

Morning brought a slight chill, but the roads and rooftops would soon absorb the sun's warmth. Honeysuckle and the scent of fresh herbs filled the air. People made their way to various destinations, some driving sheep before them, others with baskets or jugs. Habakkuk had left for the market to sell his instruments, taking Tiph'arah, Yadah, and Zimrah along to buy food and a new clay jug, leaving Rinnah and Zamiyr to care for the garden and make bread for the evening meal. Shachar had been given the task of cleaning the sheep pens and then filling them with fresh straw. Raphad still rested from his injury, but refused complete idleness. He sat in the shade of the fig tree, fashioning new sandals for Shachar.

"Do you want to start the bread or gather the vegetables?" Zamiyr asked Rinnah once Tiph'arah and their sisters disappeared through the door.

Rinnah glanced up and smiled mischievously. "Neither," she said.

Zamiyr smiled back but said, "I'll go to the garden. You start the bread."

Zamiyr walked outside, taking with her a large basket and a flint knife used for weeding. She set to work on the first row, pulling out the many new shoots that would threaten the crop if left to their own devices. She worked until the sun felt hot on her back and her legs and shoulders ached from much time in a kneeling position.

"The dough is ready and now it just needs to rise by the fire," she heard Rinnah call loudly from inside. "I will grind some more flour for Imah."

Zamiyr did not call back, not liking being overheard by the neighbors. But after a few moments, she noticed another sound. A shuffling noise came from just out of sight around the back of their house. Perhaps one of the goats had gotten free. If left alone it would destroy the garden—or worse, get into a neighbor's yard or garden and destroy theirs. She stood and stamped the stiffness from her aching knees. But when she walked around the side of the building, she discovered the sound came not from a goat, but from Shachar. She found him sitting in the shade, scuffing his feet back and forth in the dust. The worn, broken sandals barely clung to his feet. He looked up at her as she approached, stopped kicking, and he stammered an apologetic explanation.

"I have finished with the stables, but Raphad says he does not require my help with the sandals... Maybe I should go look for something else to do." He rose to his feet and shook the layers of dust from his tunic.

"You can help me in the garden," she offered, but immediately regretted asking him to do woman's work.

When he looked at her, she noticed a softness in his eyes. Though Shachar, at thirteen, was three years her senior and legally a man, he seemed younger to her in this moment.

"Very well," he responded.

Zamiyr handed Shachar the flint knife she had been using and found another. Together they knelt in silence, one on either side of the garden row, removing the undesirable plants from around cucumbers, lentils, and onions. After a while they heard Tiph'arah and the younger girls returning from the market, but her mother and sisters busied themselves indoors.

"I used to help my mother in the garden when I was a little boy," Shachar said so suddenly Zamiyr nearly jumped.

At first she could think of nothing to say to him in response, but felt she should say something. "I like gardening," she said at length. She dared then glance up and caught his eyes again. His lips curved up almost imperceptibly. She smiled back and then looked away, intent on her work. They finished their task in silence. She gathered a few early onions for their dinner and took them inside. Shachar headed off to the stables to see if Raphad needed help with anything else.

From that day, Shachar helped Zamiyr with her chores whenever he finished his early. Unlike the other girls, who enjoyed constant chatter, Zamiyr allowed Shachar to work in silence and they became quite comfortable in one another's company. At meals he sat next to her and, when Tiph'arah finished making Shachar's new cloak, she let Zamiyr give it to him along with the sandals Raphad had made.

One day Shachar joined Zamiyr where she worked on the roof, grinding grain with the hand mill. He had come up to escape the uncomfortable warmth of the house.

"Hello," she greeted him simply.

"Hello."

She ground away for several moments and then noticed he had no task to occupy his hands as he usually did when he joined her. He just sat in the shade staring out over the city roads. And then he spoke.

"I do not know what I am supposed to do here. ...I do not think your father really needs me to work for him. Raphad is healed now and already does everything around the house and stables. You and your sisters care for the garden. I cannot go down to the pasture with your father's shepherds. I could not even go for help when Raphad needed it. ...I am even afraid to go to the market," he chuckled mockingly at his own situation. "I am not in prison and yet I am."

The way he spoke made Zamiyr wonder if he really spoke to her or to himself. She was afraid to answer at first and did not know what she should say. But then he looked at her. She met his gaze steadily and saw within it a deep sorrow ...and something else she did not quite recognize. She put down the top grinding stone and slid down next to him, slipping her small hand into his larger one.

"They do not let you have friends in prison," she said in almost a whisper. He looked down at her and smiled.

Zamiyr and Shachar soon began sharing their chores as well as their leisure time. They made up games with pebbles or bits of pottery and would entertain the younger children with stories they made up.

Rinnah, used to having Zamiyr's full attention sulked, complained, and spitefully turned down invitations to join them. Eventually, though, she decided the silence Zamiyr and Shachar shared so easily was incredibly boring. About that time, Tiph'arah gave Rinnah the task of teaching Yadah to make bread. Rinnah found the seven-year-old to be easily amused by her jokes and soon enjoyed finding ways to make her laugh.

When Zamiyr and Shachar entertained the girls with games or stories, Rinnah join in, often making up a song to go along with their stories. She said the songs made the stories more dramatic. She was right. Her father took time each day to give all the girls lessons on his flute and she, in particular, enjoyed creating new music on it. But when Zamiyr and Shachar took a stroll or sat in the shade on the roof together, she found other, more interesting ways to occupy her time.

Shachar had been with Habakkuk's family for over a month. Most of the gossip about town had settled, and Habakkuk thought it time for Shachar to begin accompanying him and Raphad to the men's evening circle. But whenever he asked, Shachar politely declined the offer, seeming to prefer cleaning out the stables or sweeping off the roof. The grounds had never been cleaner and Shachar never complained, yet Habakkuk worried Shachar was unhappy. The youth did not have the peace Elohim gives His followers. He listened to the holy readings and bowed his head during the prayers—but Habakkuk never saw him pray nor had he ever requested intercession. Of course, neither did the boy have any obviously idolatrous habits. He wore no charms, owned no idols, he did not spit to ward off evil spirits. Either he had no real faith at all, or it was incredibly private.

When it was time for the Feast of Weeks, Habakkuk feared leaving him in the city alone. Usually the entire family traveled to Jerusalem to observe this sacred springtime occasion. All Jewish men over twenty were required to present themselves before the LORD and offer a sacrifice—the best of the first fruits of their harvests and herds. Habakkuk, as a Levite and musician, also participated in the worship at the Temple. He practiced for weeks in advance to be ready. Shachar, being confined to the city, could not go and so this time Habakkuk took only Raphad, leading their best spring lamb.

Zamiyr had come to understand Shachar better than anyone. Habakkuk and Tiph'arah gradually fell into the bad habit of communicating with Shachar through her. Habakkuk knew this had to stop. He still felt as though a stranger lived in his home. So, he decided it was time for Shachar to get out of the house and meet new people. The best place to start would be where Shachar would be warmly welcomed. He sent Raphad with a message for his sister and brother-in-law, letting them know that he and his family would spend that evening with them. He knew Chayil and Chemdah would be very happy to have them come, and a visit was long overdue.

Chayil, Habakkuk's brother-in-law, a hunter by trade, was of the tribe of Simeon of Beersheba. Shortly after marrying Habakkuk's sister, he had moved to Hebron. They lived only a short walk away, but until now Habakkuk had not felt Shachar ready to be introduced to the family. Now he worried he had waited too long.

When Habakkuk arrived home from market, Tiph'arah greeted him at the door as usual. Raphad had returned with a warm greeting from Chemdah. They were expected soon. Tiph'arah had already prepared a basket of sweet breads to take as a special treat, and Zamiyr busily filled another with fruit from their garden.

Habakkuk found Shachar cross-legged on the roof, working to form a flute from a long piece wood, as Habakkuk had taught him. He had already successfully hollowed it out and now dug at it with an iron knife to make air holes. He stood when Habakkuk's head appeared over the edge of the roof, but Habakkuk casually waved him back down. The boy sat again, somewhat nervously.

"Let me see," Habakkuk held out his hand for the instrument. Shachar put it in his hands and Habakkuk turned it over and over, scrutinizing it with an artist's eye. "I think this will be a fine instrument someday," he said finally. "A little more shavings must come off at this end." He pointed to the place. "Round out this edge nicely... perhaps make this hole a bit bigger..."

Shachar listened studiously to each bit of advice. His attention to detail greatly impressed Habakkuk. He still marveled that such a young man could ever have made the terrible mistake that had brought him to his door. Habakkuk finally handed back the small flute and sat beside him.

"Next I will show you how to make a drum. It looks easy, but getting the leather stretched just right is quite a challenge. In fact, it is my least favorite instrument to make. I am thinking of not selling them anymore."

"I would love to learn, Master," Shachar said with the most enthusiasm he had yet shown. "Perhaps I could learn to make them for you... and then you would not have to make them yourself anymore."

Habakkuk smiled at him. Yes, this young man definitely had promise. "Do you enjoy making these instruments?"

"Oh, yes!" he almost blurted. Then, with embarrassed reserve he explained, "I have always loved music, but my father never taught us how to make it. He is a busy man—hard working... I liked to listen to the music at the festivals, though. I think I would have liked to learn how to play the lyre."

"Then you will learn, by all means! We will start lessons soon... but not tonight. Tonight we have somewhere to go."

"What would you like me to do while you are gone, Master?"

"There is nothing here needing your attention. No, you will join our family on a visit to my sister's home."

"I would be happy to go and serve your family during your visit."

"No, Shachar. That is not what I meant at all. I would like you to join us and be one of us."

Shachar appeared uneasy. Certainly the boy had observed how Raphad interacted with this family. He served them but he also had the option of joining family activities if he wished. But Raphad was a solitary person, Habakkuk reflected. Perhaps his example did not suffice. Habakkuk felt at a loss. Was he making a mistake? Perhaps it was too soon, after all. Shachar seemed lost within himself—within his grief and loneliness. Would he ever allow himself to taste joy again?

"Come in, come in!" Chemdah cried in excitement, greeting her brother and his family at her door. She stepped aside and let the little girls dash past and embraced Tiph'arah and Zamiyr. "Hello, my brother," she said, pulling Habakkuk into a tight squeeze. "You should be ashamed for staying away so long. It is a good thing you have such a patient and forgiving sister!"

"So you often remind me," he returned, smiling and planting a kiss on her temple.

Habakkuk entered behind his wife where Chayil also greeted him with a customary brotherly kiss. Chayil then turned to Shachar.

"Shalom and welcome," he said, ushering the boy into the small family room, now bathed in lamplight and wafting with the delicious aroma of a thick, bubbling, venison stew. "I am very glad to have you in my home. You are always welcome here."

Shachar nodded and thanked Chayil, but soon located a spot at the edge of the room where he could observe the activities from a more comfortable distance.

Habakkuk's family received eager hugs and moist kisses from Chemdah's three-year-old, Siyach. Mattanah, at five, believed himself too old for such things. Tiph'arah grabbed him and hugged him anyway. Chen, at nine months old, was not yet walking but babbled joyfully upon seeing her big cousins. Zamiyr and Rinnah soon squabbled over taking turns holding her. She had large, black eyes, wispy baby hair, fat cheeks, and soft, chubby arms and legs.

Chemdah soon served food, though it took a while for everyone to settle down long enough for the blessing. Even then, Chen's baby prattle mingled innocently with Chayil's prayer.

During the meal, Yadah, having jockeyed for a position next to Chayil, often snuck a piece of his food. But soon she let him catch her.

"What is this?" he cried, feigning annoyance. "Habakkuk! Do you not feed your children? Why must this child steal?"

"She steals because she is very bad-mannered, indeed," Tiph'arah said, joining in the game. "Perhaps we should leave her here where she will learn better manners."

"No. That is a terrible idea," Habakkuk said, betraying no hint of a smile. "If we leave her here, she will turn out just like her uncle."

"Oh, dear!" Chemdah said, laughing loudly. "That would be a horrible fate, indeed!"

Yadah, let out a peal of laughter, causing her father to put his hands over his ears and her uncle Chayil to pull her into a tight embrace.

"Here," he said, pushing his plate over to her. "Eat whatever you want. I am sorry your parents do not feed you, you poor, skinny child. And now," he said, turning to the family, "I will tell you a story of my latest hunt."

"Oh, no!" Chemdah said, shaking her head and laughing. "Prepare yourselves. My husband's stories are always very entertaining. He goes out to shoot an ibex but comes home with a dragon!"

They spent the rest of the evening enjoying Chayil's exaggerated tales and laughing at Chemdah's jokes and spirited ribbing. Upon leaving their home Tiph'arah joyously complained that her cheeks ached from all the laughing.

"Even if something bad happened, I could not cry another tear. I used them all up laughing at Chemdah tonight! How is it that you and she were raised by the same parents? I have never encountered two siblings who are less alike."

"What are you saying? That I cannot tell a good joke or make up stories about hunting?"

Tiph'arah smirked. "Well… I suppose you could try…."

Habakkuk laughed at that, but later, when the children were all in bed asleep, he and Tiph'arah discussed how they felt the evening had gone for Shachar. He had remained at the edge of the party, smiling at the humor and watching the games, but somehow the joy of the evening never made it into his eyes.

"What can we do for him?" Habakkuk asked.

"We can pray, my husband," Tiph'arah answered. "We can pray."

Chapter Seven: A Distant Enemy
✡   ✡   ✡

Evening settled around them as men shuffled through the city square, greeting old friends, meeting visiting relatives, and recounting the adventures of the day. They gathered here several evenings a week to discuss various matters of importance—whose flocks had been disturbed by jackals, what the present state of the crops meant for tomorrow, births, deaths, what families were being joined through marriage, and of course, news of King Josiah. Habakkuk came to the men's evening circle and sat among them, listening to their stories. He came alone. Raphad was not quite ready to walk the distance yet.

Scanning the gathering assembly of Hebron men, Habakkuk also spotted his brother-in-law, Chayil, talking to a local merchant across the way. He also noticed Nebelah at the opposite end of the courtyard and felt immediate irritation. Nebelah's complete lack of discipline made it so that Habakkuk could not help but dislike him. At the moment Nebelah laughed boisterously with another ill-mannered man named Sebat over a new foul joke, made obvious by the obscene gestures they made.

"Could we join you, Nabiy?"

Habakkuk's irritation dissipated as he looked up into the smiling faces of his good friends, Shamar and Mishmereth. They spoke to him with familiarity and respect, calling him *Nabiy*, the Hebrew word for prophet. He welcomed them warmly and they sat, one on either side of him.

"We heard you are housing a new refugee," Shamar began, as he adjusted his robes neatly about his calves.

"Yes. His name is Shachar. He is a boy of only thirteen. Too young for such tragedy."

"I was right, Shamar," Mishmereth said, leaning around Habakkuk to catch his friend's eye. "I knew it as soon as I heard the boy's age. Habakkuk has already adopted him as part of his family." He smiled warmly at Habakkuk.

"Is it going well?" Shamar asked.

Habakkuk hesitated before answering. "It is difficult for him, but Elohim is gracious. He has a purpose in everything."

"And your family? How are they adjusting?" Mishmereth asked.

Habakkuk smiled. "Well," he said simply. "Well."

Unlike the others who had asked about Shachar seeking gossip, these men were genuinely glad to hear good news. They then asked about the trial and said they were sorry to have missed it, both having had guard duty the night before. They worked as tower guards for the city of Hebron. Tonight they would have to leave for the tower after the meeting.

Shamar and Mishmereth, rarely seen outside one another's company, were cousins and had trained for the army together as children. They worked as tower sentries, ready to warn Hebron of any danger. Though brusque and rough around the edges, Habakkuk had learned to trust them, and he greatly enjoyed their stories of heroism and adventure, told with skill and passion. Habakkuk was glad to count them as friends.

Often, if he happened to be up late, he would walk to the watchtower, climb up and talk with them as they strained their eyes through the darkness in their constant search for enemies.

"I spoke to some traders from Galilee today," the voice of Zemor, a vineyard owner, broke through the random conversations in the square. "They brought some interesting news of the Assyrians."

All voices stilled to hear the news of their dreaded enemies.

"It is reported they have finally been defeated at Haran!"

A great cheer rose from the crowd. Shamar and Mishmereth competed for who could be the loudest.

"Who defeated them?" someone asked.

"The Babylonians," Zemor answered. "They had help from the Medes and other northern peoples and from a group who call themselves the Scythians—a people from the far north, I am told. I do not know. The Babylonians defeated the Assyrians at Nineveh four years ago, as you know. And then the city of Nineveh was destroyed two years later, but now their new capital of Haran has also been crushed! It only took a couple of months to finish them off!"

Much hooting, cheers, and laughter arose from the people.

So this is how it ends for the Assyrians, Habakkuk thought. *Those ruthless, idolatrous people who thirsted for blood are finally succumbing to destruction. Prophet Zephaniah was right.*

Zephaniah, a great, great grandson of King Hezekiah and one of Habakkuk's former teachers at the Temple, had prophesied in Jerusalem years ago that the Assyrians would fall. Further, he and another prophet, called Nahum, both prophesied the fall and utter destruction of Nineveh. Zephaniah had declared that the place would be left "utterly desolate and as dry as the desert." Nineveh had fallen and been laid to waste only two years ago. But a third prophesy of Zephaniah—one Habakkuk had heard as a young man studying in Jerusalem—was the coming destruction of Jerusalem itself. Now a second of Zephaniah's prophesies had come true. What of the others?

In answer to King Hezekiah's prayer, Elohim had miraculously protected their beloved city against the Assyrians, wiping out a hundred and eighty-five thousand men in a single night. The Jews had not lifted a single sword in their own defense. Would Elohim now let the city fall?

As the men of Hebron celebrated around him, Habakkuk struggled to make sense of his feelings about the destruction of the Assyrian people. The Assyrians were in their death throes. They had been defeated at their capital and now little remained to protect them from the onslaught of their enemies—and they had many. It had been something he had hoped for, even prayed for.

Now he wondered what this news would really mean for his people. One enemy gone, or nearly so. But who would fill the void in the north? The Babylonians, perhaps. Would they be any better? Or would they be the ones to fulfill Zephaniah's prophesy against Jerusalem? Habakkuk shuddered at the thought. But he had never heard of anyone as brutal as the Assyrians. Surely the Babylonians could be no worse.

"I wish I was there to thank the Babylonian king myself," someone commented.

"Yes! Any enemy of Assyria is a friend to us," another added energetically.

"I wish I could have been there to see it," Zemor said, eager to keep his platform and glad to be the bearer of such good news. But eventually others took over the conversation. Old men recounted stories of Assyrian oppression—the same stories that had been passed down from father to son for generations. No matter how many times they heard the tales, the descriptions of the Assyrian lust for blood and skill at massacre chilled them.

The hour grew late and Shamar and Mishmereth bid Habakkuk farewell before heading off to begin their guard duties, talking boisterously and not considering whom might be trying to sleep. Chayil joined Habakkuk as other news surfaced. Someone remembered the mention of the Galilean traders and wanted to know if they were still in town. A farmer asked about a circulating rumor of a drought in Moab and worried one might be coming to Judah. Another had heard news from a traveler from the south that the Egyptian Pharaoh Psamtik I had died and his son Nekau II would take the throne. This bit of interesting news kept the men talking later than usual.

Once the meeting ended, Habakkuk walked Chayil home and greeted his sister briefly before returning to his own door. As he walked in the gathering night, he thought about what he had heard. It had been good news, hadn't it? For as long as he could remember, the Assyrians had brought nothing but suffering to Judah. Even so, he could not recall his parents showing any real viciousness against them. They had acknowledged the Assyrian's evil and the ill effects these northern, idolatrous neighbors had brought on Judah's faith, but he could not remember a single time either of his parents had actually spoken of the Assyrians in derogatory tones. It was strange to realize this. He had certainly heard enough insults hurled at their enemies from his friends, neighbors, and even the priests and prophets. And though his parents had not denied the truth of such statements, neither did they create them.

He wondered now what his father, Jeriel, would say about this new turn of events, were he still alive. Would he be glad and rejoice? Somehow Habakkuk doubted it. Although the entire town—the entire nation—rejoiced over the sweeping annihilation of their enemies, Jeriel would have remained silent. So how should he feel? He struggled with the thought. Was this Elohim's blessing, as the people believed, or something else?

Sweet, tantalizing music filled the room and drifted down the long corridors and through the open doors of the many richly furnished rooms. Tonight's coming feast had put everyone in a merry mood—especially King Nabopolassar. He walked the rooms and hallways of his palace, watching servants scurry to and fro, not letting any detail of the great festival go unattended. Dancing girls swayed and practiced while musicians intoned their best tributes to Ishtar, the great goddess of love, beauty, and war. Nabopolassar observed it all with pride. He admired the beauty of the dancing girls and male servers. He stood admiring them for a moment, letting his gaze trail over their perfect bodies. Every motion they made whispered to him of pleasure, lust, and power.

He glanced around the room. Though richly adorned, something seemed amiss about the quarters. Some day he would be able to build a larger palace—one befitting a king of his stature. Some day he would rule over all Mesopotamia, Syria, Phoenicia, and Egypt. The day was coming quickly. He smiled and grabbed a passing servant girl. She gasped in surprise but yielded. He kissed and groped her possessively before allowing her to continue with her work.

Nabopolassar pushed all negative thoughts aside. Tonight was a night for celebration! He had been gone from home too long. Now he had returned, a military champion once again. Tonight would surely secure his identity as the mightiest leader the Chaldeans had ever known.

Nabopolassar, a Chaldean prince, had been serving as governor when Assurbanipal died. Assurbanipal's death left the Assyrian and Babylonian factions to fight it out for over a year to decide who would ascend to the throne of Babylon, the Assyrian capital. Nabopolassar left nothing to chance. He rose to the top through political savvy and military might, and had worked too hard to allow his efforts to be lost in a sea of split allegiances. He was proud of his Chaldean heritage, but with him began a new dynasty and a new power in the world. He now worked not only to crush the Assyrians, but to establish his reign over what he would build into a new nation. Though they shared many of the same gods with the

Assyrians, the gods obviously favored the new Babylonians—with him as their king.

Soon the halls began filling with the voices of eager dignitaries and their wives, boasting about being invited to such a prestigious event. They had donned their finest tunics and robes—many richly ornamented with gold, silver, and jewels. Some of the robes opened to one side, curving delicately around to the front. Fringed edges swung gracefully as they walked.

The King waited in the anteroom until the special moment when he would make his appearance. His first wife, the queen, was with him. She was a beautiful woman. He had insisted on this, of course, but he had also been happy to learn she was quiet by nature. Nothing irritated him more than a bantering female.

The king and queen were both attended by servants, who fussed over them mercilessly. Tonight Nabopolassar let them. He was in a good mood. He wanted to look his best for the many important guests filling the throne room. Soon they would be led out to see the visiting dignitaries from Chaldea, Syria, Scythia, Arabia, Elam, Media, and Persia. Some came to win his favor. Others had accepted the invitation only to spy on him. He cared not. No one could hurt him this evening. They would see his power and know he deserved their respect—no—their reverence. This was only the beginning.

A great cheer arose from the gathered crowd as Nabopolassar's procession filtered into the throne room. First, a group of priests entered, ceremoniously sweeping in, carrying large, ornate bowls filled with smoldering incense that left a trail of fragrant smoke in their wakes. Next, several temple children entered, waving palm branches and dancing with lengths of delicate, colorful cloth. Nabopolassar's general and his wife followed, along with several heavily armed soldiers. Finally, Nabopolassar himself entered with his wife on his arm, surrounded by naked dancing girls and followed by a procession of richly dressed servants and personal ambassadors. The cheers grew to frenzy.

Even though everyone came dressed in his or her finest, no one outmatched the king and queen in attire. The royal tunics boasted the softest, imported linen, woven through with gold and silver threads. Small jewels dangled from the hems and danced noisily against thick, gold bracelets and anklets. The king and queen wore large necklaces and crowns made from hammered gold, embedded with jewels. The back and sides of their robes boasted even more jewels and expert embroidery from which burst fantastic imagery. The back panel of Nabopolassar's robe showed the great heroes Gilgamesh and Enkidu locked in battle with the Bull of Heaven. The front panels showed two opposing muscled lions, the sacred animal of Ishtar, rearing on their hind legs, ready to pounce on their prey.

His wife, the beautiful queen, dressed in fine linen and a robe decorated with flowers, palm trees and ibexes. Nabopolassar was the picture of victory in battle and she the personification of peace and the favor of the gods.

Once the king and queen took their thrones, Nabopolassar summoned his children and lesser wives to join the festivities. From the other side of the room another procession entered. The crowd was reverently silent as they watched the family of the king enter. At the head of the party strode the crown prince, Nebuchadnezzar. He was eighteen years old and exceedingly handsome. The young women and even the older women in the crowd giggled and blushed as he passed. His own young wife followed.

Nabopolassar stood and warmly introduced them to of the crowd. He then called his son to stand at his side. He said, "This is my son, Nebuchadnezzar II, named for the great king who ruled Babylon with dignity and honor and strength! Like him, my son will be a powerful leader one day! He will continue a great tradition of strength and power! But tonight we celebrate the gifts of the great goddess Ishtar! I, with my son at my side, have returned from battle victorious! We have defeated the Assyrians once again! Nineveh is no more and now we have crushed their petty capital of Haran! Their frightened little king, Assur-uballit II, has fled south! Soon the Assyrians will be no more, but Babylon will be the center of the world!"

The people sent up a great cheer! Nabopolassar took his son's hand in his own and raised both of his hands in the air. Then he gave his son the seat of honor at his right hand. Though it was true he and his armies had helped destroy Nineveh, he had not done it alone. He had been battling Assyrians his entire reign, but it had not been until the Medes had joined the fight that true progress was made. It was a fact he did not like to admit and liked even less to dwell on it at such functions as these. The Babylonian people needed to believe in their king and in the power of their own armies and their own gods.

It bothered Nabopolassar to admit—even to himself—that he had needed the alliance with the Medes in order to secure his kingdom. Their empire grew as quickly as his own. The Assyrians had provided a mutual enemy and showed them the profit of an alliance, without which the Assyrians would still be in control. Even now he knew peace with the Medes was beneficial to both nations. But he often wondered how long such a peace could last. He remembered the first time he had met King Cyaxares of Media. He rankled at the memory.

Some years ago, Nabopolassar had made a bold attack on Asshur, a major stronghold of the Assyrian empire located on the western banks of the Tigris River. But their former enemies, the Egyptians, had created an alliance with the Assyrians, no doubt hoping to gain control of Assyria for themselves. The Assyrians rallied during the battle and turned their forces on him in such an unexpected wave of efficiency and strength that Nabopolassar had been forced to retreat. Indeed, his armies were routed and he was forced to take refuge at Tikrit. There he found himself in a nightmare of humiliation, for the Assyrian army besieged them there. The battle ended indecisively and Nabopolassar was forced back to Babylon to regroup and plan a new strategy. At that time the Medes, heirs to Elamite power in the east, were growing in strength. Their new king Cyaxares had united their peoples even as he was uniting his. They were much alike, he realized, with a faint smile. Perhaps this was the primary reason for their distrust.

The following year, after the humiliating end of Nabopolassar's attack on Asshur, Cyaxares led his Median army down the Tigris River, sacking Nineveh and Nimrud. He then marched toward Asshur. Nabopolassar wanted to be in on the kill, but did not arrive until after the walls of Asshur had been breached. There, standing near the ruins of the hated city, he and Cyaxares met for the first time. Immediately, they found they enjoyed a mutual respect and understanding for one another, if not sincere devotion. They had agreed, then and there, to become allies and later a formal treaty had been drawn up. Soon his son would take another wife—the granddaughter of Cyaxares, when she came of age. The marriage would ratify this treaty.

But now was the time to revel in their victories at Haran. Again, the Medes had been instrumental in the Assyrians' defeat. Nabopolassar sighed. He fingered the base of his flat, cropped beard thoughtfully. He knew there were many Median ambassadors present. It was time to honor them and praise them to his guests so a favorable report would be made to their king and the alliance would not be endangered through any slight of his.

Nabopolassar called his second in command and presented these dignitaries with many gifts to take back to Media to show Babylonian gratitude for their allegiance. Next he recognized various important guests, including the Scythian ambassador. The Scythians lived north of the Black Sea. They had also joined in the battle with the Medes and Babylonians, though the Scythian's assistance had been minimal by comparison. Still, their cavalry was superb, and they had helped make the victory a decisive one. More gifts poured through his fingers to these and others to help seal their continued friendship. Maintaining peace with his neighbors was proving to be very costly, indeed.

As he finished with the giving of gifts and praises, the people cheered and the music began to play a lively ballad in praise of Ishtar. On cue, dancing girls swayed forth in a single line from a side room and danced a joyful, sultry dance for the king and his subjects. Servants entered with large basins and silver jugs filled with water. They poured water over the guests' hands and other servants came round with cloths on which to dry them.

Scantily clad servant girls circulated the room carrying rich food on golden platters. Three varieties of venison, as well as heron and quail, all expertly seasoned and roasted, adorned the trays. The guests dined on several varieties of bread and cakes made with dates, figs, and honey, and enjoyed pots of pure honey and date syrup for dipping. Cucumbers, leeks, dates, figs, pomegranates, and grapes piled high. This was the very food of the gods. Handsome young male servants carried large flasks of wine and six different kinds of beer. The music and wine flowed in harmony.

The festivities went long into the night and then continued for seven full days. Besides the music and dancing and mountains of rich foods, the priests busied themselves performing magical arts to the amazement of all who watched. They turned a rabbit into a serpent, caused bowls of food to burst into flames, and appeared and disappeared in clouds of smoke.

A royal artist troupe performed dances choreographed to represent the battle of Haran. Some of the dancers carried curved sticks, which they clashed together in rhythm with the music. As they darted and charged across the floor, their faces mimicked the passion of battle. The guests, caught up in the fury and zeal of the fight as the Babylonian victory was played out before them, reveled in the conquest.

On another evening, Assyrian captives were brought to the palace courtyard, carefully dressed in Assyrian garb, and forced to fight seasoned soldiers from Nabopolassar's army. When they were cut down and died in pools of their own blood, the crowd cheered mightily with great patriotic fervor. The bodies were dragged away to be impaled in a grisly display. The honored guests, men and women, spit on the bloodied corpses as they passed.

Later, temple priests performed dramatic renditions of how the great god Apsu and his consort Tiamat created the earth and the lesser gods. Perhaps the favorite play of the celebration was a comical reenactment of how Apsu was trying to sleep and his noisy children kept him awake. He became so enraged he wanted to kill his children. The audience laughed heartily as the wild actor ran about after the rebellious youths, brandishing an over-sized knife.

A very special performance of the epic of Gilgamesh, Nabopolassar's personal favorite of all the honored tales, had been reserved to fill the last three nights. He roared with laughter as Gilgamesh brutalized his weak, whimpering subjects. He gripped his seat as Gilgamesh and Enkidu battled ferocious beasts side by side. He wept with Gilgamesh when Enkidu died, leaving Gilgamesh alone and friendless.

Chapter Eight: Shachar and Raphad
✡ ✡ ✡

Several months passed and Shachar continued to adjust to life with Habakkuk's family. He opened up more, enjoyed working on musical instruments, and practiced playing the lyre. His progress impressed Habakkuk. The young man had even begun making up his own tunes.

Then one day a messenger came to the house and delivered a message to Shachar. He received few messages and was notably apprehensive when the messenger said it was for him. He had been right to worry. His father's business in Lachish had failed completely. No one wanted to do business with the father of a killer. His father wrote saying they had moved south to Arad, a settlement in the Negev desert. After hearing this, Shachar again withdrew to a place inside himself no one could reach. Though still polite and obliging, the fragments of personality he had begun to show again drew behind a mask.

The next morning, Habakkuk arose from a fitful sleep filled with dark, incoherent dreams. He woke with a throbbing headache. Upon seeing him, Tiph'arah told him to stay in bed and he did not argue. Perhaps he would feel well enough to go to market later. Tiph'arah brought him broth, which he sipped obligingly, though it threatened him with nausea. He turned down the bread.

The sun had climbed high in the sky by the time he felt well enough to rise. He had slept again and the headache gradually lessened to a shadow of what it had been. Voices, tinged with worry, reached him from the family room, but he could not make out the words. He rose slowly, fearing sudden motion would bring the pain back. When he entered the room, he found only Tiph'arah. He looked at her questioningly but she only said, "Are you well, my husband? Would you like some more broth and bread?"

"What is the matter?" he asked, wanting to discover the source of the worry lines on her face.

"I did not want to worry you needlessly, but we cannot find Shachar. He likely just took a walk."

"Does Zamiyr know where he is?"

"No. She was the first one I asked when I noticed he was missing."

"How long has he been gone?" Habakkuk felt the tension of concern growing in his chest, and his headache threatened from behind his right eye.

"I am uncertain, but not long. He was here for the morning meal. Do not worry. I was about to wake you, but Raphad insisted on going to look for him. He will find him."

Well, Shachar was nearly a man. He would not get lost. Perhaps he just needed a little independence. But Habakkuk could not stop the nagging worry. What if he had given up on staying in Hebron? What if he was on his way to Arad to be with his family? What if——? Tiph'arah seemed to read his thoughts.

"I checked his belongings," she confessed. "I know I should not have, but I worried he had left us. All his belongings are still there. And he took no food or water with him."

Well, that was good news, anyway. If he had planned a long journey on foot through the desert, he certainly would have packed better. Habakkuk relaxed and accepted the food his wife held out to him. He smiled, thinking how guilty she must have felt searching Shachar's belongings. But he was glad she had thought to do it. It certainly relieved much of his worry and saved him the trouble. He still felt concern for the boy, but he knew Raphad would be able to find him and bring him home.

However, all of Habakkuk's worries turned to panic when he saw Raphad carrying Shachar through the front gate, Shachar's tunic stained with red.

"Oh, no!" Tiph'arah cried, running to them. Shachar was barely conscious. Blood smeared his cheek and his left arm did not seem to be working. Raphad carried him to the bedroom and placed him gently on Habakkuk's pallet on the floor. The three of them worked together to treat and bind his wounds. Raphad set the broken arm. As they nursed him Raphad explained what had happened.

It had only taken Raphad a few moments to get to the main city gates. He thought it best to ask after Shachar there, just in case he had, indeed, decided to leave the city. But no one had seen the "young refugee", as they called him. Raphad then cut back through town toward the eastern gate to inquire there. He passed through the market on the way but did not see Shachar.

Zaqen, a lame basket-weaver with a long, thin face that displayed a prominent hooked nose, motioned him over. Zaqen claimed to have seen Shachar walking down a side road to the north of the market with some men only a few moments earlier. Raphad followed, running. He passed a few buildings but, passing a side road, he heard shouts. He turned to discover two large men violently attacking Shachar. One had the boy pinned against a wall while the other hit him again and again. Raphad grabbed the attacking man and broke his nose with a single punch. He kicked the legs out from underneath the second, freeing Shachar. The second man foolishly took a swing at Raphad, but the large Egyptian wrenched his arm behind his back, dislocating it at the shoulder. Neither of the attackers chose to continue their assault.

Raphad told this story in his usual, deep, matter-of-fact tone and seemed to have born no ill-effects from the confrontation. What bloodstains his tunic evidenced had been left by Shachar's body.

"Why would someone do this?" Tiph'arah asked in a bewildered voice as she tightened a bandage around Shachar's head.

"I did not recognize the men," Raphad answered. "But I think they must have been friends or relatives of Caphar's family. I heard them saying something about getting him out of the city."

"Yes," Habakkuk said. "If they could get him out of the city, they could legally kill him."

"That is wrong!" Tiph'arah was vehement. "The laws do not allow him to be forcibly removed!"

"But if no one saw them…" Raphad trailed off.

"Or if no one cared…" Habakkuk added thoughtfully.

"You saw them, Raphad," Tiph'arah said, wiping tears from her eyes. "And I am very glad you did. Thank you."

They got Shachar to drink some wine and then Tiph'arah gently spooned broth into his mouth. A few moments later they left him to sleep. Habakkuk and Raphad slept in the room with him to watch him through the night while the women took the roof. Even so, motherly Tiph'arah climbed down the ladder to check on him several times in the night, despite Habakkuk's assurance he would wake her if she was needed. Shachar woke often, in too much pain to sleep. When he did sleep, he was plagued by nightmares and would wake with a start followed shortly by a cry of pain the motion sent through his broken body. Several days passed before he felt well enough… or calm enough to talk about what happened. Finally he told Zamiyr why he had gone out alone and she told the others.

He had heard that morning how his master was not well. He had heard of an herb reputed to cure headaches, so he decided to go to the market to see if he could locate some. He did not recognize the men who attacked him. They told him his father had come to Hebron and waited for him by the northern city gate. So, he followed them. As he was going with them he grew suspicious, realizing that, had his father come all the way to Hebron, he would not have stopped at the gate to send messengers. He would have gone to Habakkuk's home. So Shachar had turned back, but when the men saw he did not mean to follow, they tried to drag him. And when he resisted they began beating him.

The evening of the attack, Habakkuk and Raphad visited the city governor and described the attackers to him. The governor said he would keep an eye out for the men, but many days later the assailants had not been identified.

Much time passed before Shachar recovered from his wounds. Even though most of them were not serious, he did not seem to have the will to get any better. His eyes, like his polite smiles, were empty. Zamiyr insisted on nursing him and Tiph'arah agreed, hoping her friendship with him would help him come around. But even she was not able to bring him out of his depression. He accepted her visits and obediently ate what she brought him, but still he remained distant and unreachable. Nearly a week passed this way. Shachar still slept most of each day. The rest of the time he worked in silence on his flute, carving it, decorating it, shaping it. But he never played it.

One evening, at dusk, family ate their evening meal and then gathered on the roof, enjoying the cool of the evening after a very warm day. Habakkuk played the lyre, hoping the music would float down and sooth Shachar. Tiph'arah and the girls sang a soft song of praise to Elohim along with the pleasant music.

Shachar reclined in the room. He still could not use his arm and it ached often, but his other wounds had nearly healed. He was surprised when he saw a large figure darken the doorway. Raphad had come to check on him, as he often did.

"I am well. You needn't worry," he said to the hulking man who entered the darkened room stealthily, so as not to wake him.

For a moment Raphad hesitated at the door, pondering something, but then he came in all the way. He sat on the floor next to Shachar's pallet, and leaned against the cool stone wall.

"Thank you, again, for what you did for me in town," Shachar offered the silent giant.

"You do not seem very thankful," Raphad answered bluntly.

Shachar was surprised at this and tried to stammer a response, but Raphad continued, "If you are thankful to have your life back, why do you not live it?"

"I... I do not understand," he managed.

"I will tell you a story. When I was a child, I lived with my father, my mother, and my father's first wife. The first wife was believed to be barren and so, though I was the son of the second wife, I was treated well. But when the first wife had a son to give her husband, she grew to hate me." He paused for a moment and then continued. "Both she and my father began to say terrible things to me and took to beating me. One night my mother tried to help me but, when she interceded, my father hit her so hard she died. I held her as her life slipped away. ...The next day I found my father in the field. I took a stick in my hand and I killed him. ...I was thirteen years old. I knew I could not return home, so I left that place and have never returned. I will never return."

Silence followed. Shachar finally asked, "Have you ever told the master?"

"...No," he answered slowly. "But he knows."

"But how?"

"I had been living on the roads and alleys for nearly two years before I came to Hebron. I joined a band of traveling merchants for some of that time, but I barely escaped with my life when they caught me stealing from them. I came to the Hebron market and a man caught me stealing grapes from his stand. He took me to the city governor and they began arguing about what my punishment should be. The owner of the fruit stand wanted my hand cut off. The governors thought I should instead become his slave to pay off the debt and teach me a lesson. It was while they argued that our master approached the group. I will never forget what he said. He said, 'I will take responsibility for this young man. I have been expecting him.'

"They stopped arguing. He paid them double what I owed, and so they handed me over to him. I thought this was strange because he was not much older than I. I went with him. I had nothing better to do and the governor's men still watched the city gate. But, truly, I mostly followed him out of curiosity. He said he had been expecting me. He took me to his home and gave me a place to sleep. His young wife, who was great with child, brought me some food to eat. And then a very strange thing happened. He said, 'I know what you have done. I know about your father and your mother and your life of running and thievery. The LORD has revealed it to me. I would not have brought a criminal like you into my home except that He told me to meet you today at the city gate. I could not disobey the LORD. But I will not force you to stay. If you do choose to stay I will give you a home, make sure you are fed and clothed and treated well. But you must never steal from me or from anyone else ever again. The choice is yours.'

"That night, I began packing up everything he left in the tent. I was determined to leave his house. He spoke of the gods like one speaks of a friend or neighbor. I was sure he was crazy! As soon as it was dark, I took the items I planned to steal and left the tent, but as I approached the front gate I heard growling. I looked and saw a pack of wolves circling in front of the house. How did they get in the city? I was terrified but too selfish to even warn anyone else of the danger. I made sure the gate was closed securely and went back and hid in the tent until morning. For the next five nights the same thing happened. I tried to sneak away, but the wolves paced the roads snarling and growling. Each morning they had vanished and no one seemed to know anything about them.

"During those days I learned my master Habakkuk was a Jew and a prophet. At first, I wanted to hear nothing about Elohim. I had followed the gods of Egypt. But when I called out to them in my distress they did not answer. When I left Egypt I swore I would never follow the gods—any god—ever again. But as I watched the master and learned from him, I was surprised to realize he too believed false religion to be worthless. Serving a powerless god is a waste of time... and serving evil gods is even worse. The El our master follows is a just God... but also a good God. Only a purely good God can forgive. ...I needed forgiveness. ...In time He became my Elohim as well."

And then Raphad relapsed again into silence. He rose slowly to his feet and left Shachar to rest ...and heal.

Chapter Nine: The Sparrow and the Hawk
✡   ✡   ✡

Darkness again claimed the city, and the family prepared for bed. Zimrah yawned sleepily in her mother's arms while she waited for Yadah to finish her bath. Habakkuk knew tomorrow would be a busy day as they prepared for the coming Shabbat, but he did not feel like sleeping. He still worried about Shachar, though the boy did seem to be doing better physically.

Habakkuk retrieved his warmest robe from a peg on the wall and slipped feet into sandals. Tiph'arah looked up, a question on her brow, but a look from him told her his mind. He kissed his daughters goodnight and walked out into the silent city roads. The darkness of the night surrounded him. No moon lit his way, making the stars more brilliant in its absence.

Habakkuk knew the city well, so even in the dark he easily made his way to the eastern city wall. Shamar would be there on the tower, keeping an alert eye out for danger. Mishmereth would be about a hundred reed lengths northward on the same wall, also watching from his tower. He was too far away for conversation, but in earshot of Shamar's trumpet and in sight of the signal fire used in times of emergency. Watchtowers dotted the entire city wall at strategic locations so danger could be sighted from any direction. The watchmen had the vital responsibility of warning the city of coming danger—marauding raiders, surprise enemy attacks, or even natural disasters. They also sounded their trumpets to signal the coming of morning and the onset of Shabbat.

Shamar spotted Habakkuk coming long before he arrived at the base of the tower. The soldier called down a welcome, and Habakkuk scaled the tall ladder to join his friend at one of the highest points in the city.

"How can you see on a night like this?" Habakkuk asked. "I cannot even see the base of the tower, let alone the valleys surrounding Hebron."

"I watch for movement and listen for certain sounds," he responded matter-of-factly. "Like the calls of birds that should be asleep at night or crunching brush, scattering rocks, and the like. Voices or clinking metal would be an immediate giveaway. But most of all, I watch for the signal fires of the towers out in the countryside. When lit, three of them are visible from my post. Mishmereth can see four. If an enemy approached, they could not get past the towers in the surrounding vineyards and hamlets without being spotted."

Habakkuk remained silent, straining his eyes to no avail into the thick blackness enveloping them. Even the city offered only a few sharp pinpoints of light. The lamps in the houses had long been snuffed out to prepare for night.

"What troubles bring you out tonight, Nabiy?"

Habakkuk smiled at his friend's question. Perhaps he was making a bad habit of coming here only when he felt some form of distress.

"Your eyes are able to pierce more than the darkness, I see," he responded. Then, at length he sighed and said, "I am worried about the young man who is living with us."

"The young refugee?"

"Yes."

"I heard about the attack in the shuk. I wish I had been there! I would have driven those men from the city at the point of my sword! How is the young one faring? Has he recovered?"

"Except for his broken arm, he seems to be fully recovered. ...But his heart is not right."

"He weeps inside," Shamar said, all the while moving his eyes back and forth across the dark distances before them.

"Yes," Habakkuk sighed. "Yes. But I keep praying for him."

"Sometimes that is all you can do."

"Yes."

"And sometimes it is all you should do."

They stood in silence for a moment, Shamar listening to the night sounds and Habakkuk speaking silently to Elohim. After a long moment Shamar said, "Just as dusk was upon us I saw a sparrow flying to and fro. I noticed its wild flight and looked to see what had caused its panic. Then behind it came a large hawk flying straight toward it. I could hear his large wings beating the air in a fury. The sparrow tried to get away and kept changing directions in mid-air, but the hawk was too fast and strong. It came upon the small bird with his talons extended and caught it right out of the air. ...I have never seen anything like it. Usually a small bird can get away. What does it mean, Nabiy?"

Once again Habakkuk found himself being asked to divine the signs. Just about any abnormality in nature was taken as a sign from the gods. Birds, in particular, were considered to behave according to spiritual patterns—perhaps because they spent so much of their lives in the skies, where the gods played. Many believed, by watching the birds and other animals, one could guess at the gods' plans for the future. Before Habakkuk could think of a suitable reply, Shamar continued, "I was afraid maybe we were the sparrow. ...Do you think we are going to be attacked by a powerful enemy?"

"No," Habakkuk said. "At least, I do not think we are any more at risk now than we usually are. The Edomites and the people of the Negev cannot be trusted, of course."

Habakkuk heard Shamar sigh in the darkness.

"Good," he said.

Habakkuk wondered for a moment if perhaps he should not have made any observation at all. He was not sure if he wanted the city guard to feel safe and relaxed.

✡   ✡   ✡

The next day Habakkuk asked Shachar to accompany him to town. It would be only a short morning at the market. Shachar's expression betrayed his fear of returning, but he dared not disobey. As the prophet led the way out of the house, he first kissed his fingertips and then raised them up to touch the mezuzah on the doorpost, as was his custom. The mezuzah was a small wooden box. The box contained a small, rolled strip of leather bearing the careful inscription of a sacred prayer.

Habakkuk caught a look of curiosity in Shachar's eyes.

"Do you know why we place the mezuzah on our doorposts, Shachar?"

"Yes. It is to remind us of how Elohim delivered the Israelites from slavery in Egypt."

"You are right," Habakkuk said. "But sometimes when we hear a story over and over again, we forget what it really means. Listen again to the prayer the mezuzah contains." Habakkuk recited the beautiful words of the mezuzah, "'Hear, O Israel: the LORD our Elohim, the LORD is one. Love the LORD your Elohim with all your heart, and with all your soul, and with all your strength. These commandments that I give you today are to be upon your hearts. Impress them on your children. Talk about them when you sit at home and when you walk along the road, when you lie down and when you get up. Tie them as symbols on your hands and bind them on your foreheads. Write them on the door frames of your houses and on your gates.'" Habakkuk paused for a moment to ensure Shachar was still listening. "Do you know what it means: 'the LORD is One'?"

"There is only one El whom we should worship?"

"Yes. Do you believe this, Shachar?"

"I have been taught to believe it, Master. But sometimes I wonder at the many who claim to believe in Elohim but also wear charms to please Ba'al or Ashtoreth or one of the many other gods and goddesses. Sometimes I also wonder what you mean when you talk about the Spirit of Elohim."

"Do you have a spirit, Shachar?"

"Of course."

"Do you have a mind and emotions and a will?"

"Yes. Of course."

"Elohim is this way, only deeper—with more ability and knowledge and power. Elohim also is spirit—the Spirit of Elohim. But just as you are one man, Elohim is still one El. Unfortunately there are those who have found the foreign gods appealing. The witches and false prophets tell people what they want to hear. But Elohim is not that way. He tells us only what He sees fit to reveal and then only the truth—whether it is pretty or not. And He demands a strict separation from the other gods. And who are these other gods? If they are anything at all, they are but evil spirits in disguise! And they are, therefore, unworthy of our praise. So, when Elohim tells us to love Him with all our heart and with all our soul and with all our strength, He really means all of it—not just part."

Habakkuk paused for a moment, giving time for his words to sink in. "Then Elohim talks about how we are to make sure we never forget to love him. For a long time Judah forgot. King Josiah brought us back to a place where we remembered, but this nation is far from loving Elohim as we should." Habakkuk sighed. "We have destroyed the foreign altars and renewed the worship in the Temple of the LORD. We have relearned the stories and we sing the old songs of praise. But be not deceived—evil has taken its toll on this nation. Its roots run deep and people are stubborn." Habakkuk looked at Shachar then. "This is why it is so important we remember to really love Elohim. To love Him in everything we do."

Habakkuk and Shachar moved into sight of the market place. Habakkuk saw apprehension cross the youth's face as they neared the place he had been tricked and attacked.

"One of the best ways to show Elohim you love Him, Shachar, is to trust Him."

They set up shop, and managed to sell a tambourine before packing up to return home. Though they sold little, Habakkuk gave thanks for the uneventfulness of the morning. He hoped the experience would give Shachar less reason to fear coming, and was glad to see Shachar smiling as they packed the sleepy donkey again—even if it was only because they were leaving.

They led the donkey back through the city streets, from which the dew had already dried, causing the dust to be easily stirred. They passed several of Habakkuk's acquaintances on the narrow roads. He always spoke or returned a greeting and a nod as they passed. The sounds of conversations, stubborn donkeys braying and cart wheels creaking surrounded them as they walked.

But then a new, disturbing sound reached them. It was the sound of anger and conflict. Shouts came from a house as they approached—a small house Habakkuk passed every day. He knew the man who lived here, though he rarely saw his family. The man was Sebat, one of the town leaders and one of Nebelah's good friends. That information alone would have recommended him poorly to Habakkuk; however, the man also drank much and enjoyed the company of women of questionable virtue. His arrogance and tactlessness showed in his speech and his choice of friends.

As Habakkuk and Shachar neared, the shouts grew louder. The sound of pottery breaking and then another loud crash came from the open door. A woman's cry stopped them in their tracks.

From their vantage point on the road, they witnessed an altercation occurring inside. A woman cowered on the floor, shielding her head with her arms as best she could. Sebat came up swiftly to her and stood over her yelling obscenities. He then raised his arm and hit her deftly on her left ear. She howled and grabbed at it, while doubling over. Again Sebat raised his arm to hit her. As Habakkuk saw this, his mind immediately returned to what Shamar had told him the night before. The image of the angry hawk carrying off the helpless sparrow came vividly to his mind—as though he had actually witnessed it himself.

"Sebat!" Habakkuk yelled before he even knew what he was doing. Sebat's hand stopped in mid-strike. Habakkuk saw Sebat's wife scramble away, like a wounded dog as Sebat's attention was diverted. Sebat, turning his wrath on a new target, quickly approached Habakkuk and Shachar, murderous rage contorting his face.

Habakkuk desperately searched for a way to dissuade the man's attack. Sebat came swiftly closer with long strides. Little puffs of dust arose from the pathway with each angry footstep.

"I'd like to buy your lamb!"

Habakkuk turned in surprise at the sound of Shachar's bold voice. Apparently, Sebat was surprised, as well, for he stopped mid-stride. He and Habakkuk both glanced over to the side of the house at an undersized, obviously lame lamb tied to a stick with a mercilessly short string.

"Thank you for coming out to meet us!" Habakkuk added, now that the angry monster had been distracted. The idea of engaging in a business proposal seemed to have the appropriate effect, rousing both Sebat's curiosity and greed.

"What do you mean?" he asked, unable to remove the anger from his voice.

"I see you have a young lamb over there," Habakkuk nodded toward the miserable creature, though Sebat never took his suspicious eyes from Habakkuk's face. "My young charge is interested in purchasing it from you. We were hoping you might be willing to part with it."

"What would you give me for it?" He glanced from Habakkuk to Shachar and back again.

"I have a flute here," Shachar pulled the small flute he had carved ever so carefully. "Would you consider an even trade?"

Habakkuk wanted to stop this crooked deal immediately. He knew the flute was special to Shachar. He knew it was far more than a musical instrument. It had been a therapeutic distraction from his pain and then became the source of his first songs of praise to Elohim. He did not want to see it pass to a man like Sebat. But Habakkuk remained silent.

Despite that the beautifully carved flute was far more valuable than the sickly animal, Sebat still weighed the deal carefully.

"Perhaps you would like to try it yourself before deciding?" Shachar held the delicate instrument out to him. Sebat took it and turned it over in his hands, examining it for flaws.

"I do not play," he said.

"Perhaps you would like to have it as a gift for someone."

Habakkuk knew Sebat was not in the habit of giving gifts—for any reason. However, the instrument could easily be traded at market for other goods and Sebat knew this well.

"Very well," Sebat said as though he were losing a battle. He stuck the flute unceremoniously in his belt and roughly untied the lamb. It bleated anxiously as he picked it up. Sebat shoved it into Shachar's arms—probably knowing the lame animal would not be able to walk back to Habakkuk's home. Shachar thanked him for his generosity and Habakkuk tried to engage him in other conversation—hoping to give Sebat's victim more time to escape. But Sebat was not interested in idle conversation and rudely left them standing in the dusty road holding the moaning animal.

They continued their walk back home, both consumed by their own thoughts.

Then Habakkuk said, "Thank you for thinking so quickly. It saved me from losing some teeth, I believe." They chuckled, but then Habakkuk added, "I am sorry you had to part with your flute."

"It was a good trade," Shachar replied simply.

Habakkuk looked at the mournful creature in Shachar's arms, and Shachar could see his doubt.

"I will start my own herd," he said, at which they both laughed.

After a few moments of silence Habakkuk said, "I wonder if his wife got away."

"She did," Shachar said. "I saw her go out and sneak around the side of the house to the back. Then she climbed over the back wall. He will not hit her again this night."

"Then it was a very good trade, indeed."

Chapter Ten: Passover

✡ ✡ ✡

As they passed through the last valley, Habakkuk saw the city before him and smiled. Jerusalem's gates stood wide open—her arms open to welcome the many who sought her strength and comfort. The City of David swelled with travelers from every dwelling of Judah. More and more people began passing Habakkuk and his family on the narrow road, though the entire trip had been shared with many others. The sounds of creaking wheels, braying donkeys and men's voices surrounded them. The smell of dirt and animal dung became stronger the closer they came to the city where the roads had been more heavily traveled.

Though a recent rain had dampened the road enough to lessen the dust stirred up by wheels, hooves and feet, it also caused the aromas of man and beast to become more pungent and stifling. Potholes in the dirt road became harder to avoid. Habakkuk walked in front with Tiph'arah. Zamiyr and Rinnah followed them and Raphad came last, leading the donkey on which sat the youngest girls. Mud and soil caked Habakkuk's sandals and feet, and the right side of his tunic bore a smudge where Zimrah had accidentally kicked him from her perch on the donkey where she sat with her sister Yadah. It had been a long day and a tiresome journey. And, though Habakkuk enjoyed their company, journeys always seemed longer and more tiresome when he traveled with his entire family. They would all be glad to bathe their faces, feet, and hands and enjoy a warm meal.

As he watched the activity at the gate before them, he could tell when a person of importance arrived. The city elders, who usually just sat and gossiped as people passed, would rise and welcome the newcomer with grand gestures and wide smiles. But young or old, rich or poor, the gates remained open to all. The Temple would be, too.

He loved Jerusalem. He and Tiph'arah had even been talking of moving here before Shachar came to live with them. Shachar, of course, could not live in Jerusalem, nor could he even join them on their short pilgrimage. But this time Habakkuk did not worry about the young man. Something had changed in him over the past few months. He finally seemed to feel at home with them in Hebron and miraculously his lame little lamb, after much special attention from Shachar, had grown to health. Shachar was constantly checking on the animal and feeding it only the choicest grains. Raphad even claimed Shachar had a name for it, though the Egyptian could not seem to remember what it was.

The New Year was upon them. Tomorrow marked the fourteenth day of Abib, the day of Passover. They would also stay for the Feast of Unleavened Bread, which immediately followed this sacred day. It was a time of penitent reflection upon the sins of the past year—a time to right wrongs, settle debts, and contemplate how to make the New Year a better one. It was also a time to remember.

Jerusalem had certainly endured its share of hardships and idolatry often plagued her. However, ever since King Josiah took the throne at the tender age of eight, the atmosphere changed in this magnificent city. When the King was but twenty years old, he began to purge the nation of the high places, the altars to Ba'al, the Asherah poles, and the altars to evil gods Chemosh and Molech. He traveled around the country smashing idols and shrines. He then scattered the pieces over the graves of those who had honored and sacrificed to false gods. King Josiah even opened the graves of the idolatrous priests and burned their bones on their own altars, so great was his hatred of idolatry and so intense was his desire to wipe it from Judah forever.

Perhaps the people loved him best when he went into the detestable Topheth, in the Valley of Hinnom, just south of Jerusalem where the priests of Molech reigned. There he desecrated their altars so no more of the People's sons and daughters would be burned in sacrificial fires. He even traveled into Assyrian-dominated Israel and desecrated the altar at Bethel, the high place made by Jeroboam, who had used it to welcome evil idolatry into the nation and keep the people from worshipping Eloah in Jerusalem. At the age of twenty-six, Josiah reopened the Temple of Solomon and restored the Jewish feasts and festivals. The Passover could again be celebrated after years of being forgotten. The people brought sacrifices. The priests and Levites resumed their sacred duties. The People repented and were again reunited with the El who loved them. They remembered their heritage and rejoiced over Elohim's blessings.

Habakkuk remembered it all, even though he had been but a boy when the years of the reformation began. But he was in his twentieth year by the time the Temple was reopened and the lost Book of the Law found. He remembered both the excitement and the torment as the priests read it in the assembly. Tiph'arah, only fifteen, was by his side as the words were read. She wept with him for the guilt of a nation who had lost sight of their Eloah. They had been married only two years and, though they had not yet been blessed with children, they promised one another to build their family on the one true faith. As a Levite, he was immediately required to help restore the beliefs and practices of Judaism. There was much to be done, but he relished the activity, the fervor of the people around him, and the swelling of joy in his own heart. He began training as a prophet and even achieved the highest honor of reading the Book of the Law for himself. He cherished the memory.

Habakkuk's parents also participated wholeheartedly in the national revival. Habakkuk remembered late nights in the Temple courts in Jerusalem. He remembered Chemdah—still a little girl—asleep with her head resting in his lap and her soft curls tumbling about her smooth face. He remembered his older brother Yashab's indecision about the new religious zeal. He remembered his mother, wrapped tightly in her cloak as well as an extra blanket, but still shivering. And he remembered his father.

Habakkuk's father died seven years ago. He had not been an easy man for his sons to please. Chemdah, with her bubbly nature and captivating smile, seemed to get away with anything and everything. The boys, however, often found him harsh and unrelenting. His word was law and his rod unforgiving. But Habakkuk remembered Josiah's reformation as more than just a time for national ceremonies and late nights. He also remembered it as a time of change in his own family. He remembered the strange silence that replaced the bickering and angry shouts, Yashab's worried looks, and Chemdah's oblivion. He remembered how his father's eyes changed and how the peace which settled on his father's shoulders also settled in their home. His father had retained that same peace until the day of his death. How Habakkuk missed him.

As they passed through the city gates, Habakkuk nodding to a few of the city elders he recognized, though no one rose to welcome him. Soon they would be at Yashab's door, enjoying his sister-in-law, Tanah's, cooking and surrounded by noisy nieces and nephews. Chemdah's family traveled here yesterday, which was certain to make the small house seem even smaller, the noise louder, but the enjoyment that much greater. Habakkuk also longed to see his mother again. She lived with Yashab's family, as it was the oldest son's responsibility to care for her in her old age. She felt welcome and loved here and claimed the constant activity of Yashab's eight children kept her young. Yashab, however, complained his children were turning his hair gray. Habakkuk smiled at the thought. Indeed, his brother did have more than his share of gray hair for a man of his modest years.

Yashab and Tanah warmly greeted Habakkuk's family amidst a rush of clamoring children. Habakkuk found it hard to keep them straight. Raphad did not even try.

Chemdah's three, Mattanah, Siyach, and Chen were there, vying for attention from the severely outnumbered adults. Yashab and Tanah's eight children created a constant teeming of activity and noise. Machmad, the oldest, a pleasant boy of fifteen, had been recently betrothed and would soon be leaving his family to start one of his own. He was polite and pleasant by nature. He talked easily with his elders and treated his many siblings kindly. His father, Yashab, often joked that, once Machmad married, he had to take the three youngest with him.

Metheq, another son, though thirteen and legally a man, still acted very much like a child. He was rowdy and loud, liking to play roughly with the younger ones—swinging them in the air, jumping out from behind things to scare them and the like, but he did try to be gentle and he never caused trouble intentionally. Next came three girls. Tam was twelve, just a year older than Zamiyr, Mar'eh matched Rinnah's ten, and Yediyd was nine. The five girls were always thrilled to see one another and played imaginative games whenever the austere mood of the religious ceremonies lifted enough to allow it.

Kethem, another boy, a year younger than Yadah, at seven, proved to be much too rough for her. She spent most of the time complaining he had hurt her or scared her, to the great annoyance of both sets of parents. However, Yadah greatly enjoyed Metheq's attention and squealed with laughter whenever he teased or tickled her. She enjoyed it so much she preferred to follow him around than to be with the older girls.

Ranan and Samach were identical twin boys. Only their mother Tanah seemed to be able to tell them apart without studying them first. At three years old, chaos sprang from their tiny footsteps. Their loud, emotional demands required an extra dose of attention—a thing in short supply in their home. And yet, it was hard not to spoil them. They were such beautiful little boys and always said the funniest things. Tiph'arah was particularly smitten with them, though they rarely sat still long enough for her to get her fill of hugs. To add to the fray, Zimrah and Chemdah's two oldest, Mattanah and Siyach vacillated between friendly play and tormenting one another.

To Raphad and Habakkuk's great relief, the weather was perfect for the children play outside or up on the roof. Tanah provided them with lamps, for it would soon be dark. The five girls, led by Tam, occupied the roof, while Metheq took the younger children into the yard, spinning them around or conducting tickling fights. He was so outnumbered he often completely disappeared under clamoring bodies as the children tackled him and wrestled him to the ground. Still, he greatly enjoyed being the younger children's hero and plaything. Machmad joined the adults in their preparations for the Passover and the Feast of Unleavened Bread.

Though the children and their noises left the house, Tanah and Chemdah still supplied a steady flow of banter as they washed dishes, made bread and prepared the bitter herbs. Ailsa, Habakkuk's mother, sat nearby watching baby Chen toddling to and fro, interjecting comments and advice. Tiph'arah joined in as much as she could but found it hard to get in a word. Still, she greatly enjoyed hearing about the funny things the children were doing, the latest advice for treating and dressing wounds, and who had married whom.

The men sat and talked for a while but then went outside to discuss how to butcher the lamb, despite that it was done exactly the same way each year. Though, traditionally, the responsibility belonged to the head of the household, this year Machmad wanted the honor. Finally, after much unwanted advice and teasing, his father and the other men agreed. It would be good for him to learn how to lead in this important ceremonial event before taking on his own household next year.

"I suppose if you are man enough to be married, you are man enough to butcher the Passover lamb," his father observed solemnly.

"It is hard to believe you will be a married man by the next Passover!" Habakkuk said with wonder.

"Yes," Yashab said. "Only yesterday you were running around naked, piddling on the floor."

The men laughed heartily but Machmad smiled, saying, "I do not think Raphad and my uncles care to remember such things."

"And to think, soon he could have his own children to clean up after," Chayil observed, watching Machmad intently for signs of embarrassment only to be disappointed.

"Yes, it will serve him right for all the messes his mother and I had to deal with when he was little," his father added.

"That is if he is man enough to have children," Chayil said and then added with mock concern, "Are you sure you know what to do?"

"Do not worry, uncle," Machmad answered easily without a hint of embarrassment. "I am sure I will be able to figure it out."

The men enjoyed a good laugh, and Machmad sustained several hard slaps on the back. Yashab beamed with pride at his oldest son's confidence and composure under such blatant teasing.

The next evening, just before sunset the house was once again checked to be sure all the leaven had been removed. They moved furniture and rugs and again swept and scrubbed the house vigorously on the off chance any crumbs had escaped the first cleaning. It was a merry task and the entire family worked together, singing songs. At twilight Yashab offered a prayer of thanksgiving to the LORD and then Machmad took the honor of slaying the Passover lamb while the family watched. He did it swiftly and deftly while maintaining the austere mood of personal reflection. The lamb made no sound. They roasted it whole, head, legs and inner parts, and ate it with unleavened bread and bitter herbs. They burned the leftovers in the fire that same evening.

Lamps cast soft, warm light about the cozy room as the men, women, and children found their places on the floor around the low table. Children sat in their mother's laps, but they left no one out and no one served anyone else. Everything they needed was before them so each person—man, woman, or child—could participate fully in this holy occasion. The lamb graced the middle of the table, surrounded by the bread, bitter herbs, and wine.

Throughout the course of the Passover feast, the married men took turns teaching the women and children the meaning of the ceremony. Yashab explained how the blood of the lamb symbolized the cleansing of sins. Without the shedding of blood, there could be no forgiveness. A perfect Elohim could have no communion with evil and sin could only be cleansed by death.

Chayil explained how the bitter herbs symbolized the bitterness of their bondage in Egypt. He described the difficult toil of the slaves and the cracking of the whip in such detail they imagined they were there. Habakkuk then took the unleavened bread in his hands and explained how it symbolized purity. The leaven was the sinfulness they allowed in their lives. It seemed small and harmless, but if allowed to remain, it would affect their entire life. As leavening slowly spreads throughout a loaf of bread, so sin can creep in and spread throughout a life or a people, destroying everything it touches. Elohim expected the people to be pure before Him, so He provided the way, the Passover Lamb.

Yashab recited Israel's history, starting with Elohim's call to Abraham and ending with Elohim's gift of the Promised Land. The children's eyes widened with wonder as he described Joseph crying from the depths of the well where his brothers threw him. The women blinked back tears as he told how the Pharaoh gathered the baby boys to be thrown into the Nile. The men grinned with pride as he described the victorious battle cries of the Israelite soldiers as the walls of Jericho tumbled to dust before them. Elohim's hand was in it all. By the time Yashab had finished speaking, their minds and hearts were as full as their bellies.

A quiet and reflective mood prevailed as they covered the entire floor space with bed pallets and thick blankets. The long journey, the constant activity of the day, and the long evening of talk and stories made them eager for their beds. The children fell asleep quickly. The adults carefully stepped around them making sure the children had enough covers before finding a corner for themselves.

The coming of dawn began the seven days of the Feast of Unleavened Bread. No one was permitted to eat anything made with yeast or leavening of any kind throughout the entire seven days. The first and seventh days were observed as one would observe Shabbat, so no work would be done on those days other than the preparing of food. On these days they held a sacred assembly. They woke, ate breakfast, and walked together to the Temple. A great many people filled the roads. Parents held tightly to the little ones so they were not lost in the crowds. Older children helped by keeping an eye on younger siblings. All of Judah crowded into that one city.

People gathered in the Temple courts and the priests began to offer sacrifices. These sacrifices were for the nation. Daily, they sacrificed two bulls, one ram, and seven lambs, all male and all without blemish, as burnt offerings. The smoke billowed thick and black above the altar as the fire consumed the bodies of the animals. The smell was soft and delicious at first, making their mouths water. Then the smell became bitter and acrid as the flesh burned to black ash. None of the sacrifice was retained. The fire, kept forever burning, consumed it all.

The People caught in the smoke coughed and covered their noses and mouths with their veils and head coverings or with the upper edges of their tunics and robes. Smoke stung their eyes and tears formed. The crowds shifted with the breeze. Priests continually removed ashes from the altar as the animals burned to keep the fire from being smothered. Later they would change their clothes and remove the ashes to a clean place outside the city. When the burnt offerings had completely turned to ash, a young male goat would be sacrificed as a sin offering. But they would burn only a portion of this animal. The rest would be retained for the use of the priests.

On the second day of the festival, a priest took a sheaf from the first, ripe barley of the season. There, in front of the Hebrew people, he presented it before the LORD to consecrate the beginning of harvest. Each day, the Temple priests and elders conducted instructional sessions at the Temple and, each night, music, dancing, and story-telling entertained and inspired the worshippers.

Habakkuk took his lyre and flute and spent much of each day at the Temple repairing musical instruments and practicing songs with the Temple musicians. He learned several new songs and at mealtime he returned to Yashab's house humming all the way. Yashab also had Levitical duties keeping him at the Temple for long hours. He joined with many other Levites to clean and organize the Temple and the religious articles for use during the ceremonies. He removed the litter left behind in the courtyard by the crowds, cleaned and polished the gold, silver and bronze articles, swept the altar clean, and filled the laver with fresh rainwater.

Habakkuk and Tiph'arah had mixed emotions as they gathered their belongings and prepared for the trip home. They looked forward to the peace and quiet after spending an entire week so outnumbered by children. Yet they knew they would miss Yashab's family and Ailsa. Chayil and Chemdah and their three children were to travel back with them. Chayil owned two mules and so Chemdah allowed Rinnah to ride along with Chen on one of them. They said their goodbyes and walked through the streets of the city while the morning was still new.

As they passed through the city gate, they heard a loud commotion behind them. A man, running from the direction of the palace, shouted wildly in the calm morning air to any who would listen. His shouts were intense, sharp, and distinct. His hearers stopped in their tacks, eyes wide, hands going to their mouths or covering their hearts. In a loud, intense voice, he cried, "War!"

Chapter Eleven: War!

✡   ✡   ✡

By the time Habakkuk's family arrived home, news of the war had already spread throughout town. Both men and women spoke in excited tones. Even the children began playing with sticks like swords or making slings from strings and bits of stretched leather. A large group of men formed outside the government building to hear news from Jerusalem and receive their service conscriptions.

Egyptian armies marched northward and even now entered Judean territory. No friend of the encroaching Babylonians, Egypt was bent on aiding her Assyrian allies in battle. The Assyrians, however, were bitter enemies of Judah, and King Josiah most certainly wanted to keep any aid from reaching them. So determined was he in his desire to see the Assyrians crushed, he decided to risk a confrontation with Egypt. But pro-Egyptian factions already raised bitter disputes against the wisdom of such an action. "Why should we involve ourselves in another's battle?" they argued. "Why risk losing our lucrative Egyptian trade routes and destroying the peace?" And vicious rumors circulated accusing their king of allying himself with the Babylonians.

Habakkuk's fatigue from the long walk home vanished as they passed the noisy, milling multitude. Chayil, also very interested in hearing the message from the government officials, decided to send his family on without him.

"Raphad, take the family home and make sure Chayil's family arrives safely at their door," Habakkuk ordered his servant. "I will come as soon as I have word."

Raphad obeyed. Habakkuk was glad his Egyptian servant would not have to endure any misplaced zeal from the crowds, though any would be a fool to confront a man of Raphad's stature and strength. Chayil and Habakkuk waited with the other men of the city. As people returned from Jerusalem, the group swelled with dusty, sweaty men eager for news. Finally, the governor of Hebron appeared on the steps of the government building. The crowds cheered at the sight of him but quickly quieted to hear his words.

"We are going to war!" he said in a loud voice. A riotous noise escaped the crowds, some crowing with excitement and others groaning protest. The governor quickly explained everything he knew—why the Egyptians were marching north, where they were at that precise moment, and how Josiah threatened battle to dissuade them from their course. The next morning, all Hebrew men between the ages of twenty and fifty were to present themselves at the steps of the government building to receive their orders.

It was dark by the time Habakkuk and Chayil started toward their homes. Chayil was full of excitement.

"Finally!" he said. "Those idolatrous Assyrians will finally know utter defeat! I wish I could fight them myself, but this is the next best thing." He looked at Habakkuk's worried face. "You should be glad, brother! Why do you look so solemn? Are you not glad for the chance to cut off their line of help?"

"The Assyrians certainly deserve to be crushed," Habakkuk admitted. "I could live a thousand years and never want to see another Assyrian face. But somehow it seems this battle is just another way for the Assyrians to trouble us. Perhaps I would feel differently if the battle was against them, but Egypt has been a peaceful neighbor for many years now. All that could be over."

"Tell me you are not placing your hopes for Judah in Egypt, brother!" Chayil chided. "They are a wayward group—only interested in themselves. An unreliable friend is no friend at all! Perhaps having Raphad with you for so long has softened your judgment."

Habakkuk smiled. "Perhaps I have softened toward them after knowing Raphad for so well and for so long. But even he would not encourage us to trust in Egypt. He certainly does not. I just wonder what will happen next. We have enjoyed freedom from the Assyrians, as they have been battling the Babylonians these many years. But who is to say a victory for Babylon is to be desired? Are they any better?"

"They certainly could not be any worse."

"You are probably right," Habakkuk agreed, knowing too well the torturous, bloodthirsty ways of the Assyrians.

"Well, I am going to be there extra early in the morning," Chayil said. "I want to be first in line to receive my new shield."

"I will join you," Habakkuk said.

"Are you going to join this battle, brother?"

As a Levite Habakkuk could choose which battles to join and which to pass up. Duties of faith came even before duties of battle, and the Levites were under no obligation to fight, though they often chose to.

"I do not know yet," Habakkuk said thoughtfully. "I will have to pray."

"Well, while you are praying, I will be polishing and sharpening my sword."

Habakkuk knew he was telling the truth. So eager was he for battle, Chayil would probably not sleep at all that night—even though it could still be several weeks away.

"Say a few prayers for me, while you are at it," Chayil added.

"I will… and perhaps I will sleep a few hours for you, too."

✿ ✿ ✿

Several days of bustling activity followed. A buzz of excitement and tension filled the city air. Habakkuk could only imagine what it must be like in Jerusalem. Regular soldiers, volunteer infantry, and foreign mercenaries residing in Hebron were ordered to report to Jerusalem immediately. Chayil bid his family a hasty farewell and joined the others marching north. Habakkuk had been asked if he would prefer to fight or to instead put his artisan skills to work making weapons. He chose to stay and make the needed bows, arrows, and slings. Shachar and Raphad helped.

Judah had a large infantry force; however, their chariot corps and cavalry were quite small compared to those of Egypt, Assyria, or many of the surrounding nations. The Judean armies trained primarily for defense rather than conquest, and so were well suited to the hilly, rocky terrain. Chariots and horses were often ill equipped for effective military action on Judean soil, but their infantry was well trained and their city defenses advanced.

Habakkuk joined many other artisans in their task of building suitable weapons to be sent to Jerusalem in time to accompany the army. Large numbers of men now gathered to be equipped and receive their final instructions for battle. Others worked feverishly to stock caravans with supplies for the army. Josiah would soon lead his soldiers northward to meet Pharaoh Nekau II in battle near Megiddo.

Habakkuk rose before dawn to fashion weapons. He worked quickly and often sent Raphad or Shachar to gather more supplies or take his finished products to the government building for transport. He worked long hours and returned to bed long after the sun had disappeared into the west. It was on one such night he awakened from a deep, exhausted slumber, startled by a strange noise. At first he knew not what had wakened him. Darkness filled the room and everything seemed still and quiet. But then he heard a deep voice coming from outside and scuffling. Tiph'arah moved swiftly her feet.

"What is going on?" he asked thickly.

"I do not know. I heard a woman's scream," she replied in a whisper, not wanting to wake the girls, though Zamiyr stirred on her pallet.

"What is it, Imah?" she asked sleepily.

"Go back to sleep, Zamiyr. We will take care of it," her mother replied.

Habakkuk secretly wished Tiph'arah would take care of it for him, too. Perhaps it was only an animal, after all. His shoulders still smarted from hunching over his work all day and his back and arms ached from pulling the bowstrings tight enough to create the needed resistance. But, as his senses cleared, he became curious as to whom Raphad spoke with in the dark of the night and whom had screamed. Tiph'arah waited for him to go first. He wrapped a cloak around himself and shuffled past her to the front door. In the darkness, he observed Raphad's hulking form standing over a huddled one on the ground.

"It is all right," Habakkuk heard him say. "I will not hurt you. Get up."

But the form refused to move. Habakkuk moved closer to see who had trespassed onto their property at such a late hour. In the darkness the shadowed face was at first impossible to recognize. But when she spoke he knew who it was.

"Forgive me," Sebat's wife said in quiet but desperate tones. "I meant no harm. I will leave at once."

She began to move, revealing weakness and pain. Tiph'arah, who had followed Habakkuk, moved to her and knelt to support the feeble woman.

"Please," Tiph'arah said, speaking gently. "Stay. You are welcome here."

Shachar overheard the noise and joined them in the courtyard from his tent on the roof. He crept down the ladder and stood nearby, saying nothing.

"We must get her inside," Habakkuk said. Raphad immediately stepped over to her and picked her up in his arms as easily as if she had been a child. She let out a little groan as he did so. Raphad carried her inside, and Tiph'arah ran to get her own pallet as Habakkuk lit a lamp.

When the light cast its glow on the woman's face, Tiph'arah let out a little gasp. Her face was bruised and bleeding. They immediately went to work nursing her wounds.

"Who did this to you?" Raphad asked, anger tinting his voice. But the woman said nothing. Habakkuk looked at him and shook his head slightly in a gesture that told Raphad to save his questions. Now was not the time. Besides, Habakkuk already knew the culprit. Shachar knew also and, if Tiph'arah did not, she kept her curiosity to herself as she cleaned and bound the wounds. The woman relaxed to such a degree that she nearly lost consciousness.

"She is exhausted," Tiph'arah whispered as she finished tightly wrapping a splint to the broken left forearm. "There is nothing more we can do for her tonight. She must rest. I will sit with her. You can all go back to bed."

Habakkuk and Raphad reluctantly obeyed, knowing they could do no more at present. Shachar, however, refused to leave and sat with Tiph'arah throughout the night watching over their new charge.

Chapter Twelve: The Fallen Sparrow

✡ ✡ ✡

The morning after Tuwb arrived, Habakkuk and a Shachar went to the council of elders to demand justice for the attempted murder. The council members nodded grimly and promised to bring Sebat in for questioning but the day passed with no word. Habakkuk and Shachar returned the following day only to learn no punishment had been dealt him. Instead, Nebelah stood and addressed the council.

"We all know that Habakkuk has always been an upstanding member of our community," he said, gesturing to the prophet. "But what claim can he have on Tuwb? Is she not still Sebat's wife? Is it right for another man to come into your home and steal away what is rightfully yours?"

"From what I understand," Cheresh, the priest, said, "Habakkuk did not go to Sebat's home. Tuwb came to him."

"What difference does that make, my friends?" Nebelah continued, hands wide in exasperation. "My question stands! Whether he took or enticed her away, the end result is the same! He has taken Sebat's wife and he must give her back!"

Cheresh turned to Habakkuk.

"Nabiy, perhaps you should send her back. She is not yours to keep and, although we do not look on Sebat's treatment of her with favor, she is still his wife."

"You know full well what kind of man I am," Habakkuk said, jaw tight with rage. "But, you would look on evil and allow it to continue, all the while maligning the reputations of those who would seek to prevent it." He turned his eyes on Nebelah. "If Sebat wants his wife back, let him come for her himself."

Habakkuk left them, knowing full well even Sebat was not foolish enough to face him and his enormous servant—certainly not on such feeble grounds.

✡ ✡ ✡

"Might I help you prepare the evening's supper?" Tuwb asked Tiph'arah a few days later. Sebat had not yet appeared and, despite repeated warnings from the council, they had yet to show any genuine interest in the matter, as their primary concern was Hebron's role in the war.

"Actually," Tiph'arah said, noting how winded Tuwb's voice sounded, "I was just about to call Zamiyr and Rinnah in to finish up here. I have mending to do, so I thought I would sit with you instead."

Tuwb smiled, revealing several missing teeth. "That would be nice," she said. "I enjoy the stories you tell."

"Oh, then you'll love the one about the family who attended what they thought was the wedding of a cousin, but actually showed up at the wedding of a stranger. That stranger was my brother!"

As Tiph'arah finished up her tale of comical mishaps, she failed to elicit the desired response. Tuwb offered an obligatory smile, but her eyes appeared even sadder than before.

"What is it?" Tiph'arah asked, keeping her voice low so the girls on the other side of the room would not overhear.

"Forgive me," Tuwb said. "It was a delightful story… but it reminds me of my own wedding. I did not know Sebat's temperament when I married him. And I had no doubt I would have children by now. But eight years have passed and I am no closer to having a family."

"I am so sorry," Tiph'arah said, putting a hand on Tuwb's forearm.

"I have been pregnant many times, you know. Six times. But none of my children survived the womb. This is why my husband finds me so detestable. I am incapable of bringing forth living sons for him."

"Is this why he beats you?"

"One of many reasons," Tuwb admitted. "He beat me before I became pregnant, too. In fact, I thought that, when I became pregnant, the beatings would stop… but they didn't. When I started losing our children, he punished me far more severely than he had at first. Maybe… if I give him a living son, he will stop."

✡   ✡   ✡

"He will never stop!" Tiph'arah raged through tears to Habakkuk when they were alone in the bedroom room that evening. "No wonder she has lost all her babies! If that frog beats her this way, how does he expect her body to be able to sustain a child? How can such evil be allowed to happen?"

As the days passed, Tuwb became more and more apprehensive. She startled easily and huddled into a corner each time a visitor arrived at the door, but Sebat never came. One day, word reached them that Sebat had secured for himself a position in the army reinforcements and had left town to follow the armies northward. When Tuwb heard this news she visibly relaxed.

"Come, let us go on a walk and search for flowers," Tuwb might say to Zinnah, if the child kept getting underfoot while the others tried to get work done. Or, turning to Habakkuk, on Shabbat, she might say, "Would you be so kind as to read that last passage again? I want to understand it." She closed her eyes, a look of peace on her face, during Habakkuk's long evening prayers with the family and, when he played his flute or lyre on the roof, a serene look came to her eyes—as if she was remembering a time when she had been happy.

"She is making plans," Tiph'arah told Habakkuk one night. "She is going to leave him and go to Beersheba. She has a younger brother there. I believe she has already sent him word. I saw her talking to a merchant yesterday as he passed by the house."

Habakkuk would normally have balked at the idea of a woman leaving her husband for any reason. However, hearing this, he discovered his heart and mind had softened on this issue. And, indeed, Habakkuk felt grimly certain that if Tuwb remained with her husband, she would not survive the year. Furthermore, the corrupt elders on the council would do nothing to protect her.

The next morning, Tuwb left to return to her own house. She returned later with gifts of oil, wine, and three copper bangles for Habakkuk and his family—items most certainly representing the only true wealth she owned. Tiph'arah accepted her gifts graciously, not wanting to offend her new friend, and Tuwb stayed to eat a last evening meal with the family she had grown to love. She left smiling, the light of hope kindled in her soul.

✡   ✡   ✡

Habakkuk stood at his booth in the shuk when the loud wailing began.

"The king is dead! The king is dead! Good King Josiah has fallen!"

Men and women rushed into the streets, shouting the dreadful news. Josiah, their beloved king, had fallen in the battle of Megiddo! The Egyptians had showered the Judean army with a barrage of arrows and one had fatally wounded the king. Good King Josiah died shortly after reaching his palace. Egypt had gained control over Judah.

Judah fell into mourning. Sorrowful dirges filled the air wherever Habakkuk went, and many asked him to supply them with instruments to be played in the ceremonies of mourning. A visiting Levite of Jerusalem asked Habakkuk to make new, specially crafted instruments to be used in the funeral procession of the king.

The soldiers began to return from battle. Habakkuk stood with Chemdah as she waited for Chayil at the city gates. Line after line of soldiers passed with no glimpse of him. For three days they waited at the city gates for news of Chayil. They watched the weary soldiers coming home, tearfully flinging themselves into the welcoming arms of their family and friends. They watched as the wounded were led back on donkeys. They checked the carts bearing the fallen men, whom were then handed over to grief-stricken family members to be buried in family plots. They stopped soldiers and asked for word, but no news came. Finally, as Chemdah waited nearby, Habakkuk approached a sentry he thought he recognized.

"Chayil?" the man said and then his face fell. "Yes. I know him. I am sorry, but he was struck with an arrow through the chest. He then fell from a high rock. He did not survive."

Chemdah had not heard the man's words. She sat in the shade on a low wall just inside the city gates. Habakkuk gasped.

Adonai! Oh, Adonai!

As Habakkuk approached his sister, she turned and saw him.

"No, brother!" she cried. "You must not say those words to me! It is not true! He is not dead!"

"Chemdah…." Habakkuk opened his arms to her, but she pulled away.

"No, Habakkuk! No! He is far too good a soldier! He will come home! He will come back to me! He will!"

Chemdah crumpled as shock and grief consumed her. Habakkuk caught her and helped her back to her home. Habakkuk and Tiph'arah sat with her for hours but could not penetrate her sadness. Her depression now reached as deeply into her soul as her joy once had.

Late the following night at Chemdah's home, Tiph'arah appeared from the bedroom to see Habakkuk sitting listlessly by the wall. He held something in his hands.

"What do you have there?" Tiph'arah whispered, not wanting to wake the sleeping children.

"Just a little bead necklace," he answered. "I remember it. I made it for Chemdah when she was just a little girl. I am amazed she kept it for so long."

"She was probably saving it for Chen."

"Yes… perhaps." Habakkuk drew silent and a deep sigh escaped him. The small bit of child's jewelry stilled in his hands.

"What is it, my husband?"

"I should have gone with him," he said, the words cracking with emotion. "I should not have let him go alone to battle. He was my brother—my own sister's husband! I should have been there to protect him—to fight by his side! I could have gone! But I did not. And now… now…."

"Shh! This is not your fault, husband!" Tiph'arah sat, putting an arm around him. "Even had you been there, I do not believe you could have prevented his death. Besides, how many times has Chayil faced the enemy unscathed? How many times has he battled wild animals in the hunt only to laugh about it later? Even Chemdah was eager for him to go. She knew how much he relished the fight. Chayil died doing what he loved best—fighting for his country and his king."

"But I did not see this coming, my wife. Elohim did not reveal this to me! And now my little sister is a widow. Her children—little Mattanah, Siyach, and Chen are orphans!" He fingered the tiny necklace again. "I was always able to protect her. Once I saved her from a wild dog that was about to attack her. I beat it off with a stick. Do you remember me telling you the story?"

Tiph'arah nodded with a sad smile.

"That scar on my leg came from that dog," Habakkuk continued. "But I could not protect her this time. Not from this."

That night, Habakkuk dreamed. He stood on a hill looking over a valley. The sun shone brightly on brilliant green blankets of thick, soft grass. Wild flowers of blue, yellow and pink dotted the landscape and birds sang in the sunshine. A beautiful young woman with a sweet face and strong body stood in the valley. Six laughing children surrounded her, begging her to chase them. She ran after them, breathless and laughing as she watched them dart away. She could never seem to catch up with them as they played and dashed about, smiling at her and calling to her.

Suddenly a dark shadow covered them. They stopped their happy game and looked toward the hills. Habakkuk looked, too, and saw, to his horror, a massive mountain of blood-red water rushing toward them, angry and powerful. It tore up trees and leveled mountains as its raging course advanced. The woman immediately saw she could do nothing to avoid it. She opened her arms to her children. And at the very moment her arms surrounded them in an embrace, the crimson waters overcame them.

Habakkuk woke so startled, his face, neck, and back so sweaty, he thought he had also been sucked under the violent wave. But he was in his room and even Tiph'arah had not been disturbed by his nightmare. Habakkuk immediately began to pray. But as the first words of prayer formed on his lips, a sudden realization came to him like a flash of lightning. He recognized the woman in his dream. It was Tuwb.

Habakkuk darted from his pallet and grabbed the cloak from the peg in the wall. Tiph'arah awoke at the noise.

"What is wrong? What are you doing?" she asked.

"I am going to Sebat's house. Stay with the children. I will not be long."

"Sebat's house? At this time of night?"

"I had a dream."

Tiph'arah, though foggy with sleep, understood. "Take Raphad with you, husband. You may need him."

Habakkuk leaned down and gave her a quick kiss. "I will."

Raphad awoke easily and together they took the road toward Sebat's home. But before they had gone far, they heard footsteps approaching quickly from behind. Turning, they found Shachar running after them.

"Where are you going?" he asked.

"To Sebat's home," Raphad answered him. "Our master has had a vision."

"I am coming, too."

Habakkuk nodded and the three continued through the dark roads. They came to Sebat's house and found it dark and silent. Habakkuk hesitated for a moment, unsure of what to do next. He knew he had no legal right to storm into their home. Raphad and Shachar waited patiently by his side.

Habakkuk sighed. Perhaps he should return home and come back in the morning. But then a noise came from the house. Someone scuffled about, and a light appeared dimly from the cracks in the door. Without a second thought Habakkuk dashed the short distance to their door and pounded on it. Raphad and Shachar kept on his heels. At first, there was no answer. Habakkuk pounded again.

"Sebat!" he yelled with surprising force. "Open up!"

At the sound of shuffling and objects being disturbed came from inside, Habakkuk banged again. Then Sebat opened the door a mere crack, his figure obscuring the light. He panted heavily as if he had just scaled a mountain. He reeked the bitter, stale smell of beer. "What do you want?" he demanded angrily but without his usual confidence. His voice, like his breath, was labored.

"What have you done?" Habakkuk demanded, but when the man did not respond, Habakkuk pushed past into the room. Despite the cool of the evening, the air in the room felt stifling and unusually warm.

"You have no right to enter here," Sebat whined through slurred speech, but his protest quickly waned as he watched Raphad push past as well. He even stepped aside to allow Shachar entrance.

"No!" Habakkuk cried, finding Tuwb flung into a corner under an overturned table. He and Shachar wrenched the table away and knelt beside her. Blood ran from cuts on her face and from a broken body, blotching her tunic. Only a weak raspy breath escaped her swollen lips. Shachar took her head gently into his lap and smoothed back the wisps of hair from her battered face.

"We have come for you," he whispered to her. "You will be all right now."

But he would never know if Tuwb heard him. As he cradled her, the raspy breathing slowed and then stopped. Her life slipped away.

"No! Oh, Adonai! No!" Habakkuk cried.

Sebat, face waxen and eyes bloodshot, suddenly regained lucidity and turned to flee from the room. He came to an abrupt halt and choked against the collar of his tunic, snatched swiftly from behind by Raphad.

The men dragged Sebat from him home to the doors of the governor. Habakkuk pounded on the door as he had pounded on Sebat's. First a slave appeared and finally the governor came to the door. Hair disheveled and eyes thick with sleep, he came wearing no belt or sandals. Habakkuk told him what had happened and the governor sent the slave to fetch one of the city guards.

"Go home now, Nabiy," the governor said. "Leave Sebat in my custody, and I will have one of my servants go take care of the body. Nothing more can be done tonight."

Habakkuk left the drunken Sebat in the hands of a large servant and led Raphad and Shachar away from the governor's home.

"We will return tomorrow to see justice done," he said, attempting to comfort the others. But he could not help but wonder if there was any such thing as justice.

I know Elohim sent me the dream. But why did He not warn me early enough to save her? If only Tuwb had left before Sebat had returned from the war!

He had been so consumed with sorrow for the death of Chayil and for their king, Josiah, he had barely given Tuwb another thought, assuming she had already fled to Beersheba and safety. Habakkuk was angry and amazed that his heart, already so full of sorrow, had room for so much more.

He glanced at the other men. Raphad stared straight ahead into the darkness at they walked, his face an emotionless mask. Shachar walked with head bent and shoulders slumped in defeat.

Chapter Thirteen: A Curse and a Blessing
✡   ✡   ✡

The wind blew whispers of grief and dismay. The heat returned but no one complained. Too many other sorrows occupied their thoughts and hearts. Mutterings of frustration, interspersed with angry shouts and threats, replaced the usual noisy, business-like bantering of the shuk. Habakkuk avoided it. He decided to begin building the addition he had been planning for years. Perhaps Chemdah and her family would move in with them. If so, the extra space would be needed. Raphad and Shachar, eager to help, moved Raphad's tent to a temporary position on the roof alongside Shachar's. They then began the long, arduous task of preparing the ground, purchasing the hewed stone, and planning the stages of construction.

The men had just begun to prepare the earth when a servant of the governor came to the gate and clapped loudly to gain their attention. The man wore the uniform of a guard, a sword at his side. Habakkuk was glad to see him. Perhaps, at last, there was word of how Sebat would be punished for killing his wife. Three days had passed since that night and Habakkuk had become anxious for a decision to be made.

"You are to report immediately to the government building, Habakkuk, Son of Jeriel. I have come to escort you."

Habakkuk looked at Raphad. This was not the greeting any of them expected. Habakkuk turned to the stern soldier and replied as calmly as possible, "Very well. I will come at once."

The prophet walked through the gate of his home with Raphad closely on his heels.

The guard boldly stepped into his path. "He is to come alone."

Raphad looked questioningly at Habakkuk.

"Do not worry, friend. I will be back soon."

Habakkuk followed the guard to the government building, feeling more and more like a prisoner with each step. When they arrived, he found several city elders gathered inside the main room, though too few had come to conduct a legal trial. Sebat, sober for once sat next to Nebelah, who whispered something in his ear. Habakkuk soon saw he had not been called as a witness, but rather as a criminal.

"How long have you known Tuwb, wife of Sebat?" the questions began in solemn, sly tones by the governor.

As the questions started so did Habakkuk's prayers.

"Did you find Tuwb to be an attractive woman?"

He prayed with each look, each question and each accusatory question. It was all he could do—cry out to the El who he believed would deliver him from his false accusers.

"Did Tuwb share your sleeping quarters?"

It soon became difficult to control his voice and his responses. A terrible angered stirred in his spirit. How could justice be perverted this way? Why are the righteous hemmed in by the wicked? How can a murderer sit in judgment upon his accuser? Everything seemed so backwards he wondered if this was just another bad dream. The questions went on and on.

"How long was Tuwb, wife of Sebat, in your care?"

"How many times did she come to you?"

"Did you lie with Tuwb, wife of Sebat?"

"Were there any witnesses outside your own family who can testify to your innocence?"

At one point he heard loud words and a commotion resounding from outside. He recognized Tiph'arah's voice. No doubt Raphad had brought her to plead for him. But neither was allowed admittance.

Habakkuk closed his tired eyes to the madness surrounding him and prayed again. In that instant he remembered the dream Adonai gave him of Tuwb's death. His mind then went to the story of the Egyptians and how they had endured plagues when they refused to allow the Israelites to go free. But it was one plague in particular that stuck in his mind. He saw the waters of the Nile—red and thick with blood. And he knew Elohim would provide justice at last, for they were the same waters that had rushed in and overcome the woman and her children.

All the while Nebelah whispered to Sebat, and Sebat bore a look of confidence that sickened Habakkuk. Suddenly, the prophet of Elohim could not take anymore. This was not even a real trial! If so, where were the twenty-three elders? Why did he see only guards and a governor and those evil, plotting men sitting across from him?

Habakkuk ignored the last question and stood to his feet.

"We are not through here," the governor said.

"Yes," Habakkuk said slowly and pointedly. "You are through. This is a mockery of justice and I will bear it no longer!" Habakkuk turned hardened eyes to Sebat's fat, greasy face. He looked directly at him with such intensity that an odd concern replaced Sebat's stupid smirk. He pointed at Sebat and his hand shook with rage, "That man is a murderer and yet he sits there pretending to be righteous! You all know he is guilty and yet you do nothing! You know me. You know me to be a prophet of Elohim. And I will now share with you something He has shown me. Sebat, you will not live out the year. Your crimes will not go unpunished! You may hide them from men, but Elohim never sleeps. He sees everything."

At this the governor stood and cried, "We will not tolerate threats! Perhaps you need to be reminded of who has the authority here!"

Habakkuk turned on the governor. "No, it is you who need to be reminded, governor! The LORD God—the God of Abraham, Isaac, and

Jacob—is in authority now and forever! It is He who will be my judge—and yours!"

The governor's face turned two shades of red. He stood, shaking with rage and gestured to the guards. Two of them immediately came forward and grabbed Habakkuk's arms. They were about to lead him away to be flogged, when Sebat jumped to his feet.

"No! Do not do it!" he cried out. "Let him be! I withdraw my accusations!"

Nebelah immediately tried to talk some sense in the distraught man, but Sebat waved him away insisted the guards release the prophet.

"There! You are free," he said at last through sweaty, nervous lips and threw himself in the dust at Habakkuk's feet. "Please! Remove your curse from me, Nabiy!"

Habakkuk looked the man in the face.

"I cannot remove it," he said, "but Elohim can. Turn your heart to God. Abandon your drink and cast your foreign idols into the flames. Perhaps He will forgive you."

Habakkuk turned to go. Despite his words of hope, the face watching him leave showed only despair and desperation.

No one again asked Habakkuk about the incident involving neither Sebat's wife nor Habakkuk's appearance before the council, but the entire city had heard of it. When Habakkuk received a message requesting his presence at the Temple in Jerusalem, he looked forward to leaving this city of eyes and whispers. Perhaps in Jerusalem, as he delved into the effort of creating worshipful music, he could escape… and be renewed. But one thing clutched his heart. Chemdah. She had stopped eating. She stopped talking. She stopped crying. She just stopped.

Tiph'arah's prayers and supplications filled the morning and night. But no matter how much she encouraged or cajoled the grief-stricken woman, nothing seemed to penetrate her stubborn will to die. Yashab brought their mother, Ailsa, to visit her but, when it was time for them to return to Jerusalem, Chemdah had still not awakened from her depression. Even the children seemed to have no effect on her. Little Chen weaned early with no special ceremony to commemorate the event.

The night before Habakkuk was to leave, he walked to the guard tower and climbed up to stand beside Shamar on that still night. Shamar immediately sensed the weight on Habakkuk's shoulders and wisely said little. The full moon chased away the darkness. Habakkuk stared at it until the dark spots became quite clear.

Oh, great Elohim, grant me wisdom! Should I go to Jerusalem? If I go, will I be abandoning my sister as I abandoned Chayil to go to battle alone?

Habakkuk waited in the cool breeze of the night for the LORD to answer. But no voice whispered to him from the dark. No peace settled in his soul.

I cannot leave her. She needs me. I know not what to do for her, but I will be near if she returns from her journey of grief.

Habakkuk woke before the morning trumpets sounded. He told Raphad to look after his family. He was going to Chemdah's house where Tiph'arah still remained, keeping her fruitless vigil.

Habakkuk approached the house. The uncomfortable silence marking the property since Chayil's death still clung to it. He sighed and entered the front door. But there a curious and wonderful sight caught his sight. Chemdah had finally emerged from her bedroom. She sat in the family room on a cushion by the tablemat with a bowl of stew before her. Mattanah and Siyach played quietly together on the floor nearby. Chen sat in Tiph'arah's lap sharing her bowl of porridge.

When Chemdah saw her brother enter she actually smiled at him. Habakkuk's breath caught in his throat, so great was his relief. She rose, feebly at first, and he wrapped her in a long embrace. He could see her grief was still sharp, but somehow the thick curtain of hopelessness had lifted.

Thank you, Adonai! he whispered into her hair. *Thank you for returning my sister to me!*

That night Tiph'arah, at Chemdah's insistence, returned home. Once there, she noticed Habakkuk putting some traveling items into a sack.

"So you have decided to go to Jerusalem tomorrow?"

"Yes. I finally have the peace to go. I was so worried about Chemdah I decided not to, but she seems so much better that I think I can leave now. I was amazed, really. …Whatever happened?"

Tiph'arah avoided his look and fidgeted with the fringe of her robe.

"What is it? What did you do?"

"You will never believe it! I almost do not believe it myself!"

"Whatever happened?"

"Well," Tiph'arah said, meeting his gaze, "she was not eating! Have you seen how thin she has become?"

Habakkuk nodded. His usually plump, healthy sister had become only a shadow of her former self. Her skin had grown pale, her body thin and unhealthy, and her eyes had darkened with sorrow.

"Then she stopped drinking as well," Tiph'arah continued. "She was willing herself to die! She had completely forgotten how her children need her. She even ignored little Chen. I just could not bear to watch it anymore! I hate to say it, but I became so angry with her! I have never felt such rage against a woman in sorrow! I hope Adonai forgives me for what I did!"

"What did you do? Tell me."

"I had just been consoling Chen, who was crying for her mother. And then Mattanah—only six years old—was trying to fix some of his father's arrows. He was determined to go hunting! Can you imagine? That little boy feels like it is now his duty to take care of his mother and brother and sister. Then I could only think of how selfish Chemdah was being. Her children needed her—we need her! I grabbed a bowl of porridge from the table and marched into her room. She ignored me as usual. I went up to her and I... I slapped her across the face! I cannot believe I did such a thing! But she stopped ignoring me. She looked at me with such surprise! It was as if she was seeing me for the first time in weeks—even though I have hardly left her side. And then I yelled, 'Now you eat this!' and I shoved the bowl into her lap. 'Your children need you! Do you think you are the only one to have suffered loss? Your children have lost a father and if you do not eat, they will lose their mother, too! Is this what you want? Is this what you want for Chayil's children?' And then I saw her face break! Oh, husband, it was terrible! A look of complete misery was on her face—like I have never seen before! And then she let out the most horrifying sound I have ever heard! The sob that wrenched from her was like... was like... an animal in its death throws! I grabbed her and hugged her and she cried and sobbed like—like—" And then Tiph'arah's own sobs choked her as she remembered. After a moment she continued. "Well... she cried for a long time. ...But it was good. She finally let out some of the pain. And then she ate. She ate the entire bowl and even asked for a second one! I have never been so excited to get someone a bowl of porridge! And then she slept and not once did she wake with nightmares. In the morning she hugged her children and ate breakfast with us. That is when you came in."

Habakkuk hugged his wife. "Thank you," he said. "Thank you for doing what was needed. Chemdah will forgive you and so will Elohim. He put you there with her to help her, and you did—in the only way you could."

"But I completely lost my temper and my self-control!"

"Yes. I would not have thought you had it in you. ...But it does make me afraid to ever turn down your cooking!"

And they laughed together with tears of joy. It felt so good to laugh.

Chapter Fourteen: Mourning In Judah

✡ ✡ ✡

Habakkuk met his brother Yashab and listened with great anxiety to news of the fragile state of their nation. Truly, Judah no longer belonged to the People. Egypt now sat in power.

Much talk surfaced about whether or not Egypt would maintain control. Many believed Judah would be able to break free of it soon, for Pharaoh Nekau II was too busy facing down the Babylonians and bolstering the armies of Assyria to care much about such a small nation. Even now, Pharaoh and his army camped at Riblah, in the land of Hamath, too far away for a hasty return.

Today a great ceremony was to be held in Jerusalem, for the crowing of a new king of Judah at the allowance of Pharaoh. But great conflict surrounded the appointment of this new king, for he was Josiah's firstborn son, the crown prince. Neither was he the second or even the third. Josiah's fourth son, Shallum, had been handpicked by Pharaoh Nekau II, for now succession of the dynasty was subject to Egypt's desire. Shallum was son of Josiah and Hamutal, of the city of Libnah. As king, he would no longer be Shallum, but Jehoahaz, meaning "Jehovah seized," for the LORD had seized Judah and handed her over to another.

Though much celebration usually accompanied the crowning of a new king, Judah was not in a celebratory mood. They had just buried their beloved king in his tomb. Weepers and mourners still wailed for him in the Temple, in the palace, and on street corners. The prophet Zephaniah now served the people for the last time, honoring his fallen cousin and king. He had arranged for the Temple musicians to play dirges throughout the streets. Soon they would play joyful, lilting choruses—regardless of the weight in the hearts of the musicians and the people. They would dry their eyes and lift their heavy hands to cheer their new monarch. Surely, the new king too, having just lost his father, felt the same sorrow and emptiness that made their souls wan and desolate.

Habakkuk and his brother walked through the vast Temple courtyard toward the Temple. They headed to an inner room to listen to the musicians practicing for the evening's ceremonies. As they approached the massive Temple, they heard a man shouting from the broad steps to the crowds. He stood tall and thin, dressed in the garments of a priest. Startling to behold, his eyes looked on the People with an intense and piercing gaze.

He cried, "This is what the LORD says: If you do not listen to me and follow my law, which I have set before you, and if you do not listen to the words of my servants the prophets, whom I have sent to you again and again (though you have not listened), then I will make this house like Shiloh and this city an object of cursing among all the nations of the earth!"

He repeated this message again and again as the people passed, and several stopped to listen. As Habakkuk and his brother approached, they could see the listeners were becoming angry. Habakkuk and Yashab heard their grumbling remarks. "Why does this man plague us with curses on this day of mourning? Who is he to suggest we are not worthy of Elohim's blessings? How dare he say we will become like Shiloh?"

Shiloh, a place cursed by Elohim, was not mentioned often and then only in hushed tones. After the Israelites entered and conquered Canaan all those hundreds of ages past, they set up the Tabernacle at Shiloh, a city about a day's journey north of Jerusalem. Shiloh resided in what had become the Northern Kingdom shortly after Solomon's death. But even before the days of Solomon, Shiloh was utterly destroyed.

The Philistines, long-time enemies of the Israelites, had found a new reason to be angry and embittered toward the Jewish people. They captured the Ark of the Covenant and foolishly placed it in their own idolatrous temple in Ashdod in front of a large statue of their god, Dagon, only to discover a shocking sight the next morning. The statue of Dagon had broken into pieces. His head and his hands fell from the statue, crashed to the ground, and lay on the floor in front of the ark of Elohim. Dagon bowed before a more powerful God.

Soon afterward, a plague of tumors struck the people of Philistia. They feared the El of Israel was punishing them. They moved the ark of Elohim to the Philistine city of Gath, only to bring the plague to the people of that city. Finally, they set the ark and a large guilt offering in gold on a cart hitched to two milk cows and sent them out of the city. In this way, the ark returned to the Israelites.

But even though the people of Philistia healed from their tumors, their anger continued to burn. Soon they retaliated against the Israelites by destroying the city of Shiloh. They attacked this city, looted and burned it, and killed all in their path. They carefully avoided the Tabernacle for fear of calling down Elohim's curses on themselves yet again but they destroyed the city so completely, Shiloh remained empty and deserted for years. In time, it became a symbol of Elohim's displeasure with the Israelites for carelessly and foolishly using the Ark of the Covenant as a magic charm.

Habakkuk asked his brother, "Who is that man?"

"His name is Jeremiah. He is a priest and he claims to be a prophet of Elohim."

"You sound as if you do not believe him."

"Many claim to be prophets these days."

"Do you know him?"

"I have met him a few times."

"And you did not think him to be trustworthy?"

"Oh, I suppose he is as trustworthy as the next man." Yashab did not seem eager to continue this conversation, but he added, "He and King Josiah were very close, from what I hear. But I never found him to be… well… very approachable. He finds more fault in people than good and he has very few friends—if any."

"Even fewer now," Habakkuk observed as the crowd became more and more hostile in their remarks.

Some of the men talked conspiratorially to each other, gesturing angrily toward the prophet on the steps above them. But surely the people of Jerusalem would not cause trouble for the man while he was on the very steps of the Temple.

Habakkuk took a last glance at Jeremiah.

"He is heartbroken," he observed, almost to himself as they passed by the prophet and the angry listeners at his feet. "But if he was close to Josiah, it is no wonder." Another though struck Habakkuk. If this Jeremiah was a true prophet of Elohim, why had Elohim allowed Josiah to die when such a close friend was His prophet? Why had He not used Jeremiah to stop the king from such a foolhardy mission?

Yashab read his thoughts. "I guess I doubt he is a prophet, because if he was, Josiah might still be alive today. But when the Pharaoh of Egypt came through, Jeremiah was gone. He was nowhere in Jerusalem. Josiah was left without counsel when he went to battle. Would not Elohim have kept Jeremiah here to warn him? I just do not understand."

But then Habakkuk was reminded of how he was not with Chayil when he died, either. There had been no warning—no message from Elohim, no vision, no dream that would have kept Chayil alive. Elohim had been silent. Perhaps Elohim had been silent before Jeremiah, as well. Maybe this prophet felt as lost and confused and abandoned as he did.

✡   ✡   ✡

Habakkuk stayed in Jerusalem throughout the coronation, joining the crowds gathered at the Temple. There Jehoahaz stood before them with High Priest, Azariah. In the presence of the people, the priest placed Josiah's crown on the Jehoahaz's head. The crowds gathered closer to the Temple steps and strained to hear the next words of the Azariah, for now he approached the new king with a bound scroll.

Azariah's face was a mask of solemnity. First he handed the new king the scroll. He placed it in Jehoahaz's right hand, but kept one hand upon it.

"This is the Law of Elohim, the Great El Shaddai, the El of Abraham, Isaac and Jacob. These are the words of the LORD our Elohim who brought us out of slavery in Egypt and His commandments to us, His people. As you become king, you become Elohim's vessel in Judah. Do you vow to follow Elohim's Law and lead the people of Judah to also follow it?"

"I vow it," Jehoahaz said with equal sobriety.

Azariah released the Book of the Law. Next he turned and received a second, smaller scroll from the hand of one of the lesser attending priests. He placed this scroll into Jehoahaz's left hand, again keeping one hand on it, and said, "This is the Testimony, the regulations governing the king's duties and conduct as prescribed by the covenant between Elohim and His chosen king to His people. Do you vow to follow these statutes as king of Judah?"

"I vow it."

Azariah released the second scroll and then turned to another priest on his left. From this man he received a small silver vial. He held the vial over Jehoahaz's head and said, "I anoint thee king of Judah, Elohim's chosen one."

He tipped the vial and poured a small amount of oil onto Jehoahaz's head.

Until that moment a solemn, reverent silence had prevailed among them, but as the oil seeped among the black curls of Jehoahaz's head, a great cry arose from the people.

They shouted, "Long live the king! Long live the king!"

Again and again they chanted the words until the walls echoed with it and the ground reverberated at the sound.

Finally, the entire throng formed a great procession from the Temple to the palace. Once there, they followed Jehoahaz and his entourage of priests and officials to the throne room. Jehoahaz walked solemnly, determinedly forward. He approached the throne, where he was flanked by priests, High Priest Azariah on his right. Finally, he sat on the throne, and again the crowd cheered and chanted. The king had assumed power.

Habakkuk did not stay for the rest of the ceremony. A long line of dignitaries and officials had come to present themselves to the king, one by one, to declare their loyalty. Habakkuk was not an official of the court; therefore, he was not required to swear his allegiance to the king in this public arena. Another festival had been planned for that evening, though, so Habakkuk decided to accompany his Yashab and Yashab's family to enjoy the music, the dancing, and the mountains of food.

But even in the midst of the celebration, Habakkuk knew the People still mourned in their hearts. He thought again of Jeremiah, the mourning prophet. As he and his brother made their way back to Yashab's home, he found himself looking for Jeremiah, but the tall man with the piercing eyes was nowhere to be seen.

✡   ✡   ✡

Habakkuk said his farewells to Yashab's family and headed south on the road from Jerusalem and Hebron, a road he had traveled many times before. He felt as eager to get home as he had been to leave. He missed his family and he was anxious to see how Chemdah and her family fared.

The day began with a glorious morning. When he started out, it had been cool but, as afternoon settled among the hills, the sun grew fierce. Habakkuk soon felt it heating the back of his neck and shoulders. He kept his eyes on the path in front of him to avoid the sun's intense rays.

As he walked, he reminisced about the many joyous occasions that had brought them to Jerusalem in the past. He imagined Tiph'arah, walking by his side. He liked traveling with his wife, though he generally preferred to leave the children at home. He found her thoughts and comments entertaining—what she wanted to see in Jerusalem or humorous stories about the girls—and he enjoyed the release of sharing his plans, worries, and visions. But traveling alone had its benefits, too. It gave him time to think and time to pray.

Habakkuk liked to pray throughout the day—just let his thoughts and questions be shared in the presence of the El he felt all around him. Habakkuk usually enjoyed a comfortable relationship with Elohim, but today many questions plagued him. Turmoil in his soul made it difficult to know where to begin. So, instead, he hummed a tune he had made up long ago to accompany a prayer. It was a song of worship.

After watching his shadow grow to his left for a couple of hours, he finally decided to rest and eat. Besides his money pouch, he also carried a small satchel of food Tanah had generously prepared. It contained a loaf of wheat bread, cheese, a few dates, and a skin of wine. He had eaten a piece of flat bread and a bowl of vegetable stew for breakfast and usually did not indulge in an afternoon meal, but walking made him uncommonly hungry.

Perhaps he would not eat all of it, he thought. Perhaps he would only eat half and save the rest for his evening meal. This would keep him from being glutinous and wasteful.

The path ahead wound through a mountainous pass, but a few paces ahead a smooth place off to the left under a spreading tree looked welcoming. Near the tree sat a boulder. The tree would provide him shade and the boulder would provide him privacy and something to lean against. He would be unable to see the road if he took advantage of the tree's shade, he realized, upon approaching. The thought made him a little uneasy, but he reasoned no one traveling the road would be able to see him, either, so he was safe enough.

His stomach growled as he positioned himself cross-legged in the shade and pulled open the cords of the satchel. The soft bread and the flavorful cheese and dates smelled delicious. Perhaps he would eat all of it, after all. He laid his meal on the rock and knelt beside it. For several moments he thanked Elohim for the meal and his family. He thanked Elohim for a safe journey and asked for continued safety. Then he prayed for his new king and his countrymen—for their deliverance from evil temptations and for their hearts to be faithful to the LORD God.

After giving thanks, he took his food pouch and eased himself into a comfortable spot at the base of the tree. It was nice to get the sun off his back for a while. First, he took a drink from the wine skin and found it refreshing and relaxing. He munched the bread, cheese and dates, thinking of the chores he needed to do once he arrived home.

Before Habakkuk finished his food, he heard the sound of voices. He peered between the rock and the tree trunk and saw two men coming from Jerusalem. He did not recognize them and they had not seen him, so he returned to his meal. The cheese was quite good and so he savored it. Once his food was gone, he washed it down with a last swig of wine, and returned the remainder to the satchel and stood. As he tied the pouch back onto his belt he heard raised voices.

Angry voices and one loud, desperate cry emanated and echoed among the rocks in the mountainous pass ahead. Habakkuk ran toward the noise. The two men who had passed by earlier stood over a young man beating him with sticks. The man's cries weakened as the blows sapped his strength and will to fight back.

"Stop!" Habakkuk yelled. He ran toward them, yelling. When the thieves saw Habakkuk charging them, they took off. First, however, one of them tore the cloak from the young man's body, and the other gave him one last blow across the back of the head with a large stick. The victim lay sprawled and motionless, his face in the dust.

Habakkuk ran to kneel beside him. With slow, careful motions, he rolled the man onto his back. The stranger inhaled, straining to breathe, and groaned. Habakkuk sighed, relieved to know the man yet lived, but a large gash marred the left side of his forehead. Other than scratches, Habakkuk found no other obvious wounds, but he was no physician. Tiph'arah was much more skilled than he at caring for the sick or injured.

Habakkuk retrieved his wine skin and put it up to his mouth. He dribbled some of it in between the bruised, dusty lips. As he did so, he noticed the man wore a circular amulet on a cord around his neck. Usually such charms were worn next to the skin and hidden from sight. The struggle must have drawn it out.

The injured drank, wine dribbling down his cheeks and chin onto his neck. Habakkuk poured what remained into the wound on the man's forehead. A groan of pain escaped his lips, but after a few moments he revived.

"Thank you, my friend," he muttered feebly. "You have saved my life." He rolled over and slowly pushed himself to a sitting position. Habakkuk helped him, waiting for the dizziness to slip away.

"I am sorry I was unable to stop them from taking your cloak."

The man groaned again, but then said, "It was no fault of yours." He groped about a bit. "I think they took my money pouch as well." He sighed, but said, "I am deeply grateful for your assistance. Because of you they did not get away with my life."

"Do you know those men?"

"They are strangers to me," the man replied. "I am journeying from Jerusalem to Juttah. I planned to stay the night in Hebron and then travel the rest of the way tomorrow."

"You will stay with me and my family. You will stay until you feel well enough to make the journey home or until your family can be informed of your condition and come retrieve you."

"Thank you," he responded weakly. "My name is Zaham."

"I am Habakkuk."

"Habakkuk?" Suddenly the expression of the young man changed. He recognized the name, Habakkuk was sure. Zaham noticed his exposed amulet and self-consciously tucked it back inside his tunic.

Chapter Fifteen: A Tearful Farewell

✡ ✡ ✡

"Do you know me?" Habakkuk asked, a little embarrassed to have forgotten this man—if he had ever known him.

"No, no," Zaham said quickly. "I do not know you, though, I have heard you are a prophet."

Habakkuk wondered wryly how far the news of his pronouncement on Sebat had traveled. But he said, "Are you well enough to walk? I can help you. The distance is little now. In a few hours we will be at my home." Habakkuk, now eager to be on their way, stood and offered a hand of assistance to his new charge. This place was unsafe and would attract even more thieves once darkness fell.

"Yes. Let us leave this evil place," Zaham said.

Habakkuk helped Zaham to his feet and they headed south. At first, Habakkuk allowing him the man to lean against him, one arm across the prophet's broad, strong shoulders. But as they went, Zaham's bruised muscles loosened and he began to walk on his own.

"Are you from Juttah?" Habakkuk asked. "I have friends there. Perhaps you know them."

"Uh… no. I am just visiting friends."

"How long will you be staying?"

"Not long."

Habakkuk's attempts at conversation did little to dispel the awkward silence, so he eventually gave up. His longing for home increased. He would have been there by now if those thieves had not attacked this man.

As they came in sight of the wall of Hebron, Zaham suddenly found his tongue. "I am very grateful to you for your great service to me. I have caused you to get home late and probably to neglect your duties, as well. For this I apologize."

"No apology is necessary, Zaham," Habakkuk replied, graciously. "I am eager to introduce you to my family and get you some good food and rest. You should feel much better in the morning."

"Again, I thank you," Zaham said, but now his voice became stuttered and uneasy. "However, I have remembered I was supposed to meet a friend here in Hebron. He will ask me to stay at his home, and he must be worried about me by now."

"Ah, well, I will take you there, then. What is the name of your friend? It is likely I know him." Habakkuk's curiosity piqued. He wanted to know who had shared information about him to this man.

"He lives not far from here," Zaham said. "I cannot keep you any longer from your family. I will go there on my own."

"It is no trouble," Habakkuk insisted. "You are hurt and I should like to make sure no more harm comes to you."

"No, truly, I will go on by myself. Thank you again for your trouble. Shalom to you, friend." Zaham turned away and began walking down a separate path toward the west end of the city. Habakkuk could not understand this man's secrecy. Perhaps it was his idolatrous upbringing and knowing Habakkuk was a prophet of Elohim made him uncomfortable.

Zaham was not the first to have this reaction. Did he really have a friend in town expecting him? Habakkuk doubted it. But Zaham certainly had no intention of going to Habakkuk's home.

Habakkuk sighed and let it go. He felt weary and eager for his wife's company. The longer they were married, the more he missed her on these little trips.

Habakkuk rounded a corner and the scent of burning incense accosted his senses. As he walked the narrow path between homes, the smell grew in intensity, as did his apprehension. Someone nearby was worshipping an idol. The hair on the back of his neck stood up.

As he passed a darkened threshold, a hand reached out and grabbed the sleeve of his tunic. Startled, he stopped to see who had taken hold of him. Habakkuk stood in shock, looking upon the naked body of a woman he did not recognize.

Quickly, Habakkuk turned his face away, but it was too late. He had seen her. All of her.

"Who are you?" He demanded. "Why do you cling to me?"

"I am a priestess of Anath. You have found favor with the great goddess of this place. She would give you a gift."

"I want nothing of her!" Habakkuk cried, trying to pull away. The witch held him with surprising strength.

"Am I not beautiful?"

She was. She was very beautiful.

Habakkuk pulled back harder, but the naked woman kept her grip on him and stepped from her doorway into the alley—out in plain sight of anyone who might pass by. Desperate to release himself from his grip, he lowered his hand from his eyes and, trying not to look at the rest of her body, grabbed her wrist to wrench her fingers loose from his sleeve.

"Let go of me, woman!" he cried, but she was close to him now. Too close.

"Anath wants to give you her blessing," she said. "She promises great bounty, Man With The Hard Eyes. All you need do is come in to me. Find pleasure and blessing in my arms."

"No!" Habakkuk said, and pulled away. He quickened his steps and fled, leaving her behind.

As he dodged out of sight at the next road, he thought he heard her laughing. Wild and hysterical, like the woman in his vision. It followed him, scratched at him as he ran, flew above and around him like an evil spirit.

He heard the insane, wicked laughter, even as he opened the gate of his home, despite the distance he had put between himself and Anath's priestess. But as Habakkuk crossed his own threshold and saw Tiph'arah waiting for him at the door of their home, the laughter ceased.

Habakkuk rushed to his wife and plunged himself into her arms, burying his head in her neck, hair, and shoulder.

"My husband," she said, instantly alarmed. "What is it? What has happened?"

"I… I missed you," he said, voice muffled and heart pounding.

"I missed you as well," she whispered. "But you must tell me what is wrong."

"I will. I will tell you… someday."

✡   ✡   ✡

The building project proved time consuming but also medicinal. It felt good to have a new project and watch the foundations come together. When finished, the house would consist of four rooms surrounding a courtyard. He also hoped to build a permanent stone staircase to the roof in place of the wooden ladder, but that project would have to wait.

One busy morning, Habakkuk and Raphad went into town to trade for bitumen to be used to mortar the stones together. While there, Habakkuk overheard drunken laughter emanating from a nearby courtyard. He turned to see Nebelah and Sebat. Sebat snorted in laughter at a joke, but when he saw Habakkuk looking his way, his smile suddenly faded. He swallowed hard. Nebelah returned Habakkuk's stare with a mocking smirk.

They have done nothing! Sebat murdered his wife and the city officials have done absolutely nothing to him!

But Habakkuk knew Sebat would not escape judgment for his crime. The thought brought him comfort.

The sun beat upon their backs as they worked through the heat of late morning. Soon they would stop to rest during the hottest part of the day. Tiph'arah was inside preparing them a refreshing snack of cucumber slices, grapes, and flat bread. Zamiyr and Rinnah had gone to visit Chemdah and take her some vegetables from their garden. The younger girls, eager to help their father, worked to fetch water for the mortar.

Habakkuk and his servants perched on the new walls to fit long wooden planks across them to bear the weight of the roof, which would also serve as extra living space on warm days and nights. With each plank dropping into place, the family's excitement grew. Habakkuk grew more and more anxious to be done and was reluctant to stop. But when the little girls complained of the heat, he finally relented and began his descent down the ladder. Just as he started down, however, he glanced Zamiyr and Rinnah coming down the road toward home. He immediately noticed the worry on their faces and in the gestures of their hands as they talked together.

"Chemdah is leaving," Rinnah blurted when they came within earshot.

"What? What do you mean?" Habakkuk asked his second daughter.

"She is taking the children and moving to Beersheba."

Chayil still had family in Beersheba and no doubt they had invited her to live with them. It was their duty and they would want their grandchildren, nieces, and nephews close by. He looked at the partly finished addition to his home and sighed. His sister and her children would not be living in it.

In the three months following the coronation of King Jehoahaz, disturbing rumors began to circulate regarding questionable royal alliances, warring political factions, and unwise government management. Former court officials, known to be corrupt, somehow made their way back into the palace after having been removed from duty during Josiah's reign. The people raised questions about Jehoahaz's intentions and even his competency to rule. Many worried whether the well-loved and respected army general would continue in service. If he left, would the army follow the new appointed general?

Lines crossed the foreheads of the people as they fussed with one another about the deteriorating state of their vassal nation and the rising crime rate. But even as these concerns were raised, the coming of a new message caused gossip to be replaced by sincere concern for their king. Pharaoh Nekau II, the new ruler of Judah, had ordered King Jehoahaz to meet him at Riblah. Their king had no choice but to go.

Habakkuk went to the men's evening circle to hear the news coming from the capital.

"They say the Pharaoh's general marched right into the palace with his soldiers and dragged King Jehoahaz right off the throne!" Zaqen said.

"Don't believe everything you hear, old man!" Nebelah retorted.

"It could be true," Habakkuk heard his large friend Mishmereth say from across the courtyard. "The King is only twenty-three, and I hear he is just a little man."

Laughter erupted from various parts of the courtyard, but was quickly muted into humbled silence when Priest Cheresh spoke with surprising fire, "Have you already sold your allegiance to these Egyptian overlords? Where is your pride?"

Though Cheresh continued to berate them, Habakkuk's eyes followed something at the edge of the crowd. A dark figure slid between and behind the oblivious listeners. The figure seemed hovered about and then moved slowly and unnoticed between the people. Then it turned slightly and Habakkuk recognized her. It was Zanah, the witch. He wondered what she was doing but then Cheresh again arrested his attention with fresh, disturbing news.

"Our king, young though he may be, is now a prisoner of Pharaoh!"

The announcement drew the desired response. Cheresh's stomach protruded with satisfaction as anxious questions flew at him from various parts of the courtyard.

"What have they done with him?"

"I heard no such thing!"

"What happened?"

"What are they going to do with him?"

"He is already gone," Cheresh said dramatically and mournfully. "He was taken from his home and his family and the country he loves to live in Egypt—a prisoner to the man who killed his father!"

"Are we going to pursue them?" someone asked.

"No. Word from Jerusalem is the Pharaoh has already selected King Jehoahaz's successor. Soon we will have a new king."

Again Cheresh enjoyed the barrage of questions, all demanding to know the identity of the man who would take the throne.

"Pharaoh has chosen Eliakim, Jehoahaz's older brother, Josiah's second son," he answered them. "He will be our new king."

A moment of near silence descended as the people absorbed this new information. Then everyone began talking at once. Cheresh tried to regain their attention, but eventually gave up.

Habakkuk caught enough of the clamoring conversations to gather that Eliakim was twenty-five years old and reputed to have more natural administrative ability than his younger brother. However, many disturbing rumors surfaced regarding what kind of man Eliakim was. Unlike Jehoahaz's mother, a native of Judah from the Levite city of Libnah, Eliakim's mother, Zebudah, was from Rumah, a city in Israel to the north, now long dominated by Assyrians—a land of idol worshippers. Throughout his youth Eliakim had become known throughout the nation as spoiled, unpredictable, and intrigued with magic.

"Perhaps the responsibility of the throne will calm him," Zemor said on a hopeful note. The men thought on this and many nodded, not wanting to offend the respected vineyard owner with their blatant disagreements. But then Zaqen, who enjoyed the forgiven tactlessness of old age and lameness, spoke what everyone was thinking.

"Power never makes the power-hungry better. It only makes them worse."

In the days following, Eliakim did indeed assume the throne of Judah. His name was changed from Eliakim, meaning "Elohim will establish", to Jehoiakim, meaning "Jehovah will establish." Pharaoh Nekau had chosen the name not only as a sign of his control over the king, but also of his goodwill toward his new Judean vassals, specifically honoring the El of the Jews and the El of Josiah. But the Judean people wondered how long this honor would last.

The day of Chemdah's departure arrived too soon. Chayil's older brother, so like him in appearance, but unlike him in demeanor, came to lead Chemdah's family south. Habakkuk and Raphad helped them pack her belongings into a small cart. The children climbed on top, sitting on crates and bundles, excited about the journey. Chemdah walked with Habakkuk and his family beside the cart all the way through town, out the city gate, and about a rock's throw along the dusty road before they stopped to bid their final farewells. Tiph'arah masked her grief well until that last moment when she and Chemdah clung to one another at their last parting. They wept freely. Then Chemdah climbed onto the wagon and turned to watch her brother's family fade from sight as the creaking wheels robbed her of them.

Chapter Sixteen: Lean Times
✡   ✡   ✡

Along with a new king, Pharaoh Nekau II also bestowed on Judah a heavy levy. He demanded a tribute of a hundred talents of silver and one talent of gold paid to Egypt. One talent equaled three thousand shekels of weight and, since Judah had a relatively small population, each man was sorely put to contribute to this warlord's fee.

Habakkuk, having just finished the addition to his home, had little more to give. He took half of his flock and sent Shachar to the Sheep Gate to sell them. Then he packed his instruments on his mule, and he and Raphad made the two-day journey to Gaza, where he hoped trading would be more successful. There they found even more evidence of the Pharaoh's influence and control, but since the city was a major center of trade he managed to sell most of his instruments. Eager to be on their way again, they collected what remained and headed back home.

As Habakkuk and Raphad approached the house, he saw a mule he did not recognize tied just inside their gate. Tiph'arah appeared in the doorway and then a tall, dark man came up behind her. At first Habakkuk did not recognize him. Worry clenched his heart. What was this stranger doing in his house with his wife? What had happened in his absence? But as he and Raphad approached, he recognized their visitor. It was Sakal, Shachar's older brother. Habakkuk had not seen him since the trial and now wondered what had brought him up from Arad to Hebron.

Habakkuk greeted him warmly, but still felt uneasy about his presence there. He should not be there while Habakkuk was away. But Sakal put the prophet's fears to rest quickly.

"I only just arrived a few moments ago," he said. "I was about to leave to spend some time at market while I waited for your return, but now that you are here, perhaps I will stay."

The look on Tiph'arah's face confirmed what Sakal said and indeed he still appeared tired and dusty from the journey.

Habakkuk replied, "Certainly! We are honored by your visit! We will butcher a lamb for our dinner this evening."

As Tiph'arah and the girls prepared the meal, Habakkuk's stomach began to knot with hunger but, when Sakal spoke of the reason for his visit, Habakkuk forgot his hunger.

"I must admit I have come with sad news," Sakal paused and glanced at Shachar, who sat nearby. "Our father is quite ill," he said and then continued. "As you know, we moved to Arad so our father and I could find work. Business was finally beginning to improve. We felt great relief after struggling for so long. But then my father began coughing and having trouble breathing. The illness persisted for many weeks and every remedy we tried has failed. He is getting worse. ...We fear he will not live much longer."

Habakkuk listened with deep concern as Sakal spoke. Though Sakal was a man of little emotion, his eyes belied the calm in his voice. Habakkuk saw a deep worry there, a hopelessness.

"We are very sorry to hear of your troubles," Habakkuk said. "But I am grateful you have come to bring us this news. We will keep your father in our prayers."

At this, Sakal looked grateful, if not expectant. They finished their meal, talking of plans and worries. Sakal felt confident business would continue to flourish, for he had already taken over management and, in a few years, his own son would be old enough to learn the trade. Na'veh, their mother would be well taken care of if Ivah passed on. By the time they finally retired, the oil in the lamps was nearly consumed.

Sakal left the following morning, anxious to be back at his ailing father's side after seeing his brother and delivering his message. Tiph'arah prepared him a meal for his journey, and Sakal bowed deeply as he left. It reminded Habakkuk of Ivah. He sighed. He suddenly regretted his eagerness for Ivah to leave during their previous visit. Now they might never see him again.

Shachar had said little during his brother's visit. He spent a good deal of time on the roof whittling flutes from bits of wood, but no music floated down to them.

"He wants to go to his father," Zamiyr said when he did not join them for dinner. "He is very worried."

Later the girl took a plate of food to his room and returned with half of it gone, but Shachar did not come out. Habakkuk entered and found him sitting in near darkness, turning a newly made flute over in his hands absentmindedly. He jumped to his feet at Habakkuk's approach, but Habakkuk motioned for him to sit.

"I have been thinking..." Shachar began timidly. "My enemies are busy with their own affairs and far away in Lachish. Now that my family is in Arad, perhaps it would be safe for me to go and see him."

Habakkuk sighed. "You must distraught with worry for your father."

Habakkuk could barely make out Shachar's nod in the dark room but heard the young man swallow hard.

"I wish it was safe for you to go," Habakkuk continued, "but we both know there is no guarantee your enemies will not find you. If they have heard of your father's illness, they may very well be waiting even now for you to leave the city."

"How can I worry about my own safety when my father is on his deathbed? If I do not go now, I may never see him again."

"But if you do go, we may never see you again."

Shachar hung his head.

"I know I am not your father," Habakkuk continued, "but you have become like a son to me. I do not want to lose you. My family would no longer be complete without you."

Shachar remained quiet for a long moment. Then he cleared his throat and said, "I will remain. I know my family will understand… and I do not want to cause him to worry about me. …And thank you. You have been a father to me… when I needed one the most."

Habakkuk spent the following day in the hills near Hebron cutting and gathering wood for new instruments. He would also use the skin of the lamb they had slaughtered to make leather tambourines and hand drums. As he walked, searching the ground with keen eyes, he hoped to find a ram's skeleton so he might salvage the horns, but he found only stones and brush. Finding some wild herbs good for stews and medicines, he picked them and tucked them gently into his satchel to take back to Tiph'arah.

He enjoyed his day scouring the mountainsides. Though he did not find everything he needed, the country was peaceful and open. He walked slowly, enjoying the sun and breeze and the sounds of nature.

Elohim is here. He is everywhere. He is above, below and all around. He courses through this land like a strong wind. Unseen but always present.

Habakkuk thought of Chemdah and her children, now far away. He thought of Shachar, trapped inside a city of people who scorned him, if they thought of him at all. He thought of Tuwb and how everyone had already seemed to forget how horribly she had died… and lived. He thought about Judah and how so many were already forgetting what Josiah's reign had stood for—honest zeal for the LORD. But Elohim did not forget.

As Habakkuk drew near the city gates, men scuffled about and whispered strangely. All eyes were upon him but, at first, no one spoke to him. He shot several of them a questioning look. What had happened? And then a fear jumped into his heart. Was his family well?

"What has happened?" he asked Zaqen, who sat on lame legs weaving a basket in his lap. He was the only one who did not fear Habakkuk, and Habakkuk now depended upon his blunt honesty.

"Sebat is dead," he replied matter-of-factly, his calloused fingers never slowing with their long-memorized tasks. "It happened just as you said it would. They are all afraid you will put a curse on them, too."

Habakkuk, though relieved his family was well, felt annoyed at the superstitious paranoia of these men who were supposed to be city leaders. He had not cursed Sebat. Sebat's own actions called down Elohim's judgment. Habakkuk merely saw it in advance.

"You do not seem afraid," he said with a half-smile to Zaqen.

"Why should I be? Any god in his right mind would not curse me. I am cursed already!" He laughed a wheezy laugh and slapped his thin, withered thigh. "I would be a waste of time and energy!"

Habakkuk chuckled but his smile dulled at the sight of Nebelah coming swiftly toward him.

"Ah, here comes the Wild Bull of Heaven now!" Zaqen said with amusement. "He has been pacing the streets, calling on the gods and spitting all day long! You had best watch out! He is sure you murdered that infernal wretch he called a friend."

Nebelah ran up to them, but despite his bloodthirsty rage, did not address Habakkuk directly. Instead, he stepped aside and grabbed the governor by the sleeve and began pointing and yelling accusations.

"I demand this evil sorcerer be put to death! He has killed my friend, a pillar of this community! You all heard him call down a curse on Sebat's head and now he has made it come true!"

"Calm down, Nebelah," the governor answered. "You know Sebat's death was an accident. Five people saw it happen."

Habakkuk was at a loss to understand what had happened. However Sebat had died, it must have happened this very day. Zemor, standing near the governor, saw Habakkuk's confusion and explained.

"This morning Sebat was in front of his home fastening a cart to his donkey. Something spooked the dumb animal and he took off down the road at a run. Sebat's hand became tangled in the harness and he was dragged with the cart on top of him. ...He was alive when they got the cart stopped, but barely. He could not speak or move. He soon died of his injuries."

"Habakkuk made his God bring down curses on Sebat! You all heard his curse! He is at fault! He knew this was going to happen! He caused the animal to be frightened!" Nebelah raged.

The governor and the other elders looked at Habakkuk as though awaiting some explanation.

Before Habakkuk could answer, Zaqen spoke up, "You superstitious fools! Habakkuk has been gone all day in the hills. I saw him leave this morning and he has only just returned! Do not act surprised, Nebelah! You have been waiting for him all day yourself! Do not think we could not see you lurking about in the roads. And if his God killed that murderer, Sebat, who are we to question it?"

"I am merely a prophet," Habakkuk added. "I do not tell Elohim what to do, I can only relate what He shows me. Sebat's death is on his own head! I only gave him warning. If he had repented and asked Elohim to spare him, this might not have happened!"

Nebelah would not be dissuaded from his desire for vengeance, but the elders found no legal ground with which to charge Habakkuk, so he was free to return home. But that evening he received a disturbing visit from Priest Cheresh.

"I heard of what happened to Sebat… and what happened at the city gate when you returned from the fields," Cheresh said.

"Yes, Nebelah blames me for Sebat's death," Habakkuk replied without shame.

"I know you to be a good man, Habakkuk," Cheresh said slowly, mentally assembling his words. "I know you are a prophet of Adonai and have never been wrong in your prophecies and warnings. …But perhaps you should …avoid calling down …heavenly judgment on others."

Habakkuk's brow drew together.

"I did no such thing," he replied. "As a priest of Elohim, you must know I have no such power! I merely warned him of his fate if he did not repent!"

"Yes, yes, of course," Cheresh said. "But you know how superstitious these people still are! If you call down curses, they will begin to fear you. Is that what you want?"

Habakkuk set his jaw. "I gave him a warning from the LORD," he responded firmly, eyes hard. "Nothing more."

Cheresh shifted uncomfortably where he sat in Habakkuk's family room and then waved a careless hand in the air.

"Of course! And you did him a favor, no doubt, by giving him an opportunity to make things right."

"What? Men have no power to make such things right. One can only repent and throw oneself at the mercy of Elohim—beg Him to bring healing and forgiveness."

"But Sebat did not repent, did he?" Cheresh continued. "All you really succeeded in doing was frightening the people. Now they think you are a sorcerer, not a prophet."

"They are mistaken."

"Yes, certainly! You know it and I know it, but perhaps next time you will think twice before relating bad news that cannot be averted anyway?"

"I only speak what Elohim tells me to speak. I only obeyed, and if He asks me to speak again, I will."

Cheresh sighed as though dealing with an ornery child.

"Very well, Nabiy," he said, leaving Habakkuk unsure whether he used the term with respect or sarcasm. "I have only come to speak to you as a friend, to be a help to you. I do not want to see you lose business over this or see your family suffer."

Cheresh rose and Habakkuk saw him to the door. As Cheresh left the house, Habakkuk turned with a sigh and his eyes caught sight of Tiph'arah in the threshold of the bedroom. From her expression, he saw she shared his frustration.

Months passed and winter seemed to linger as the nation tried to recover from the heavy taxes Pharaoh exacted from them. Habakkuk's business suffered, but not due to superstitions, as Cheresh had warned. For who could trade for musical instruments when they had barely enough to acquire the grain they needed to feed their families? Thankfully, Habakkuk's flock sustained them.

When spring came, Tiph'arah planted extra seeds in her garden, and Habakkuk and Shachar's flocks, though considerably smaller, showed signs of promise for the coming year. They were healthy and amorous, and Raphad believed thinning them had given the young males a new freedom and a keen desire to increase their numbers again.

But in the midst of their struggles to replace what had been taken by Pharaoh, a rumor circulated that King Jehoiakim had exacted quite a bit more than the Pharaoh's true levy. With the extra funds flowing in, he broke ground for a newer, much grander palace to be built for himself. As his heralds traveled the countryside with conscription notices for the recruitment of Judean citizens to serve on this new building project, the king threw lavish parties for himself at the traditional palace in Jerusalem.

Jehoiakim also chose to please himself with as many young virgins as he could find, and regularly added beautiful young girls to his harem from all parts of Judah and the surrounding tribes. Whenever Jehoiakim's steward came to Hebron, Tiph'arah wisely made sure Zamiyr had plenty to occupy her inside the house. For, Zamiyr exceeded in beauty.

Chapter Seventeen: Death, Comfort, and Planning
✡   ✡   ✡

Summer was nearly upon them. The flax harvest was nearly at an end and the barley harvest had begun. Habakkuk decided to go to market only once a week to sell instruments and, instead, focus on increasing his flocks. If anyone wanted to buy an instrument during the week the men at the city gates and in the shuk would surely point them to his home, for he was the only person in town who made them. And so he was home when a stranger from the south came looking for him.

"Are you the nabiy named Habakkuk?" he asked.

"Yes."

"I come with a message for you from Arad," he said and began digging in the drawstring bag at his waist.

Habakkuk, instantly concerned, watched the man retrieve a piece of etched pottery. As he feared, the pottery bore the dreaded words relaying Ivah's death.

Habakkuk had a terrible task ahead of him. He gave the man a bit of copper for his trouble and went to the roof to pray. He sat beneath a woven flax awning and read the message again.

"Ivah, son of Challamiysh has died this fifth day of the new moon. Sakal and his mother, Na'veh will visit in two months' time."

✡   ✡   ✡

Dusk had fallen. The sky remained cool and cloudless. The ladder groaned softly as Zamiyr climbed slowly, timidly to the roof. She paused and peered over the edge. Shachar was there, sitting on the floor, leaning back on his hands and staring up into the sky, which was just now beginning to release a few of its stars from their daytime captivity.

"Join me," he said in a near whisper without shifting his gaze from the blue-gray ocean of sky.

She climbed the rest of the way and walked silently to his side where she assumed the same position as he. She followed his gaze. A few wispy gray clouds coasted ever so slowly in the evening breeze and a young moon glowed on the horizon.

"Do you think Elohim can see us?" he asked.

"My father says Elohim watches all we do," she answered.

"But what do you think?"

She thought a moment before answering. "One night I had a terrible nightmare. I dreamed a lion had broken into our home and was about to eat me up. I cried out—or I think I did—but when I sat and looked, my family still slept. I was too afraid to speak and I had no one to comfort me. Then I remembered Abba had said Elohim never sleeps. So I prayed—not out loud—just in my thoughts. And in that moment all of my fear slipped away and I knew I was not alone. …Yes. I believe He is watching us, even now."

Shachar was silent for a moment. "I am having a terrible nightmare, too," he said. "But I cannot wake up."

"But you are not alone, either," she said and slipped her hand into his.

He turned then and looked at her. Despite the sorrow in his eyes, he smiled at her and squeezed her hand. "Your father talks of Elohim as if he can hear Him talking back."

"I think he can."

Shachar looked back at the darkening sky. "…I wish I could."

"I think you can, too… if you listen."

"I do not know how."

"Ask Elohim to show you."

They slipped into silence. A few birds made a lazy path across the sky to find their final roosts for the night. The young people heard Tiph'arah calling from below for Zimrah to come inside for bed and Zimrah's answering call from somewhere in the yard. Then her quick, scuffling footsteps rose from the beaten earth.

"Your family is wonderful," Shachar said quietly to Zamiyr. "But I do not know what I would do here without you."

"Why would you have to be without me?"

"Someday soon you will be betrothed and then married. Then you will go away," he said, sadness in his voice.

"Then I will marry you," she said with a child-like matter-of-factness that surprised him. He looked at her and she looked even younger and softer in the dim light.

The thought had never occurred to him, but now it seemed so right, so natural. Suddenly, a nugget of hope—and longing—lodged itself within his breast. And as he sat there, her hand still grasped tightly in his, a large part of his pain, loneliness, and loss slowly gave way to something new.

Sakal and Na'veh arrived in just over two months' time, as promised. Sakal, unchanged, was the same, tall, polite young man they had met before but Na'veh had aged considerably since her last visit. She sat in the family room with Tiph'arah sipping warm broth and pouring out her troubles. Her tears spilled like wine from a rip in a wineskin.

Na'veh did not have a close relationship with Sakal's wife. Since moving to a new city, her visit with Tiph'arah offered her the first chance to truly release her grief over the death of her husband. But afterward a long talk, she visibly brightened, began to notice Zimrah's sweet little songs, and took a new interest in Shachar's welfare, wanting to know every detail of his life in Hebron.

Sakal, polite in a manner not unlike his father's, bowed more than necessary, made eye contact while nodding his understanding to each statement directed his way, and offered profuse thanks at each meal and at each offer of drink. Broad shouldered and muscular, his difficult labor showed upon his frame. More comfortable out of doors, maneuvering around so many people in the small room made him look awkward and ill at ease. So, Habakkuk invited him to sit with him on the roof to talk.

They began speaking of how the city was changing, but then Sakal said, "I have not spent much time in Hebron, but I believe it will be a good place for Shachar to live. Your kindness and generosity have helped him a great deal. He is no longer the same person he was when he came."

"He has grown up a good deal in the past two years," Habakkuk agreed.

"Yes, that is because he has been greatly blessed by your family …but somehow Caphar's curse still found us," he said with a sigh in a casual manner.

His words recalled to Habakkuk's mind that ugly moment when Caphar, father of Me'ah, shouted hateful curses upon Shachar, his family, and his offspring. Habakkuk had not linked the curse with Ivah's strange illness and untimely death. But had Caphar's curse really worked? Did the evil gods roaming this place attack Ivah and bring about his illness and demise? Sakal seemed to think so. And while Habakkuk knew neither god nor man had such power over Elohim, he had heard of magical arts and the casting of spells that evidenced an uncanny, if not completely reliable, power. He wondered if Ivah had truly known the one Elohim. He claimed to be a practicing Jew, but his superstitious questions suggested he had been influenced by the surrounding idol-worshippers—many of whom resided within the cities of Judah.

When the men returned to join the family indoors, Habakkuk found, as Na'veh's mood improved, Sakal's and Shachar's spirits also lightened. By the end of their second evening in Habakkuk's home, they were actually joking together and reminiscing about childhood pranks and mischief. It was the first time in the two years Shachar lived with them Habakkuk witnessed Shachar's delightful sense of humor and infectious laughter. He suddenly had permission to release his guilt and sorrow and find his true person again. The curtain had been thrown back and the sunlight warmed them all.

Habakkuk watched him with wonder and delight. It brought such joy to his soul to see this young man finally released from his captivity—and to think it happened in the midst of such a sorrowful occasion! Elohim certainly worked in unexpected ways.

But as Habakkuk watched and laughed with Shachar and his family, he noticed something else. Zamiyr sat at Shachar's side, as usual, but there was something new in the way he looked at her. And as Habakkuk looked he could see she, too, seemed different somehow. He decided to speak to Tiph'arah about it that very evening, but as it turned out, he was not the only one to have noticed.

Tiph'arah cleared away the bowls from before them and sent the girls off to bed. As Zamiyr rose to leave, Habakkuk noticed Sakal watching her. He still talked through a mouthful of bread, but his attention bothered Habakkuk.

When night claimed Hebron, Habakkuk pulled his pallet close to his wife. The girls were already fast asleep in their usual places and the sounds of their soft breathing added to the calm of the night. As he lay down, she slipped an arm across his chest and he sighed at the comfort her touch brought him.

"Did you enjoy your evening, husband?" she whispered.

"Yes, very much," he whispered back. Then after a pause and a tired yawn, he said, "Shachar seems like a new man."

"Yes, Elohim be praised!"

"…Tell me of Zamiyr. She seems… different."

"She is different. She has become a woman."

Habakkuk sighed. "She must be betrothed soon, I suppose."

"Yes."

"I have thought of it often of late… but every young man I know does not seem to be… to be…"

"…good enough," she finished for him.

"Yes. But tonight… I began to wonder about Shachar."

"What about him?"

"Well, I do not know. …I just thought... but I might have been mistaken."

"You thought Shachar was in love with her?" she said very softly.

"Did you see it, too?"

"I thought I did, yes."

"He is a good man," Habakkuk said thoughtfully. "And he should have been betrothed, if not married, by now. But, to be honest, I hope he is not in love with her! It would make her life much harder, and I do not know what kind of a future he could provide for her. He is a prisoner in this city. I do not even know if his father already arranged a marriage for him before his death."

"I would be surprised if he had…. Certainly, Sakal or Na'veh would have told us. But there is still time for Zamiyr. We must keep praying until the LORD shows us the right man for her," she said and snuggled closer.

He wrapped an arm around her so she fit perfectly against his side, her head resting on his shoulder. And then another thought hit him and he groaned.

"But in these times it is going to be very hard to plan a wedding—even if we did find the right man. I have sold everything of value to pay our taxes! There is nothing left for a dowry."

Tiph'arah said nothing. In fact, she barely breathed, waiting for him to go on. He sighed.

"But Elohim will provide. He always does."

And then Tiph'arah relaxed against him and the softness of her skin against his caused his exhaustion to drift away.

Chapter Eighteen: An Offer

✡ ✡ ✡

On the afternoon of the third day of Sakal and Na'veh's visit, the women knelt in the garden and Shachar and Raphad worked on cleaning out the sheep pen. Sakal approached Habakkuk and asked if they might go on a walk. Habakkuk sensed Sakal had more on his mind than seeing the sights of Hebron, so he nodded and together they walked through the city, out the city gates, and strolled along the well-worn footpaths through the southern valley.

Sakal talked casually of family and business until they were out of earshot of any townspeople. As the town faded behind them, Sakal's mood suddenly changed from light to serious—even timid.

"Forgive me," he began. "I am still young and inexperienced in these matters. I do not want to offend you with what I am about to say."

"Please, do not worry. Speak your mind."

"It is just... well, it is up to me now to secure my younger brother's future."

Habakkuk, fairly sure of what Sakal was about to say, waited patiently for him to go on.

"I would like to ask you if you might be interested in allowing your eldest daughter, Zamiyr, to marry Shachar. —I know there is much to consider," he went on hurriedly, almost apologetically. "He is not in a very good situation here, so if you are not willing, please say so—and perhaps you might instead be willing to suggest another young woman from this city for him. She is young and very beautiful, so I am sure you will have no trouble finding a suitor for her. In fact, you probably have fathers already coming to you seeking a wife for their sons, and, and...." Sakal stumbled to a stop.

You are right. You are not very good at this, Habakkuk thought, but stopped walking and looked Sakal in the eye.

He wavered for a moment in what he was about to say as he silently prayed for wisdom. Did Shachar have a strong enough faith in Elohim to be a good husband and spiritual leader for Zamiyr? He considered Shachar and realized how different he was from the frightened, depression-ridden child who had come to them two years ago.

Shachar had become a skilled craftsman and a worthy musician, but the gentleness of his speech and manner belied the strength in his heart. Habakkuk remembered how he had tried to save Tuwb from her husband's fists, and how deeply he had mourned her passing. Shachar was no longer a lost child. He was a man of strength and compassion and, yes, a man capable of deep faith.

And so it was with great joy and sincerity he replied, "Shachar would make a very good husband for my daughter… and he is already like a son to me. I would be very pleased if an arrangement could be made on their behalf."

Sakal, visibly relieved, sighed and a happy smile appeared on his lips. He grasped Habakkuk's arm and Habakkuk clapped him warmly on the back and kissed both of his cheeks.

"You have made me very happy!" Sakal said sincerely. "And, if you do not mind me saying so, I believe they will be very happy together. They seem to already have a deep affection for each other."

"Yes. They have been like brother and sister since he came, but I think that love has grown into something more. They are quite close. Zamiyr knows his thoughts even before he speaks them."

"How very fortunate for them. Their friendship will be a great benefit in their marriage."

Habakkuk wondered if Sakal's own marriage was a comfortable one as they turned and started back toward Hebron.

"I suppose we must now discuss the bridewealth to be paid and the date for the wedding," Sakal said in a more businesslike tone, though excitement still evidenced in his voice. "As you know, we are just starting out in Arad and, though business has been increasing, we have not fully established ourselves there. My father's illness and the national taxes have also been a burden, but I believe in a year or two, we could save enough for the occasion. …Your daughter is still quite young, but Shachar is already a man of fifteen. He should be wed soon."

"I could also use the time to save for a dowry and for the wedding expenses," Habakkuk replied. "And, as you said, Zamiyr is still too young— only twelve. Though many other girls have married at her age, she is not yet ready."

"So, how much would you consider to be a fair amount for the bridewealth?" Sakal asked with a respectful amount of timidity.

"The customary amount is about thirty shekels of silver," Habakkuk replied. "I believe it is a fair amount."

"No, no," Sakal said seriously. "I would not consider giving such an amount."

Habakkuk paused in his stride at this perplexing rebuff.

But before Habakkuk could respond, Sakal hurried on, "I would not consider giving any less than forty shekels. Given the circumstances of Shachar's… situation, I think it only fair. Zamiyr must have security."

Habakkuk relaxed and smiled.

Sakal then added, "Zamiyr is very beautiful and she is a capable woman in the home. My mother praises her gentle manner and her skill at cooking and weaving and tending the garden. She will be a good wife for my brother and a blessing to our family."

Habakkuk nodded his agreement and smiled at the kind reflection on him and on his wife. He, too, had noticed Na'veh's watchfulness and heard her frequently praise Zamiyr, though at the time he had not considered the basis of her observation.

Sakal continued, "I will begin saving at once. We have family who may also be willing to contribute, and my father had a little silver saved before he died. I suspect by this time next year we could make a legal betrothal between them."

"And perhaps by then, I will be able to let go of my daughter," Habakkuk chuckled at his own paternal pride and nostalgia.

"Yes… I understand. I have a daughter of my own. Zamiyr and Shachar will live in Hebron, of course, but where in Hebron will they live?"

"They could live with us," Habakkuk replied. "He is already my apprentice, and I have just added two new rooms to our home. There is plenty of space for them until such time as he decides to build his own house."

"You are too generous, Nabiy," Sakal responded.

"This is my daughter we are speaking of, after all."

When Habakkuk and Sakal returned to the house, they found Zamiyr leaving with a basket to go to the market for her mother. Dark hair pulled back from her face, a few childish strands had slipped free and danced with her every movement. She smiled at them politely, holding open the gate for them to enter, eyes bright and youthful.

And in that moment, in her simple act of anticipating their need, Habakkuk saw in her the woman she would become—thoughtful, diligent, beautiful.

Habakkuk stepped aside to allow his guest to enter first but did not take his eyes from his daughter. She grinned up at him, still holding the gate. He took her chin in his hand and kissed her forehead. Her smile broadened. For now, at least, she was still his little girl.

END OF BOOK ONE

Habakkuk's Plea

Evil Persists

Scrolls of the Nevi'im Book II

S. E. Thomas

Following, you will find a sneak peek at what is in store next for Habakkuk and his family.

Chapter One: A Warning

✡ ✡ ✡

608 B.C.

Habakkuk blinked in the early morning sun. He turned his head toward the sound and smell that had invaded his dreams. Incense. A muttered prayer. Even now, his neighbor, Pinon, knelt on his rooftop before a small smoking bowl, eyes closed, hands raised to the empty morning sky. Blood ran down his arms from cuts along his wrists.

"Nikkal-wa-Ib, Nikkal-wa-Ib, Nikkal-wa-Ib," he rocked back and forth, chanting the name of the Canaanite goddess of orchards and fruit. "Nikkal-wa-Ib, I seek your blessing. Nikkal-wa-Ib, Nikkal-wa-Ib, Nikkal...."

✡ ✡ ✡

Tall grasses rippled in the breeze. The sheep and goats grazed lazily, completely ignoring the sound of the shepherds' laughter. Three trained dogs guarded the flocks, trotting to and fro around the edges, keeping alert to strays. The sheep ignored the dogs until one lamb happened to stray a little too far and was immediately attacked with barking and nipping. The offending animal scrambled awkwardly back toward the flock only to immediately forget its transgression in favor of fresh grass, instigating the barking and nipping again.

So much like us, Habakkuk thought, watching them.

Habakkuk had joined his hired men for the day and sat among them under a large oak tree within sight of the flock. They shared the meal of bread, cheese, and apricots Tiph'arah had sent with him.

Shepherds were generally a boisterous and unkempt group, prone to uncultivated, unpredictable behavior and unsavory joking. Habakkuk's men were no exception. However, with their master about, they tried doubly hard to modify their speech in deference to his moral leaning. They hid their superstitious tendencies with far less success, spitting to ward off evil spirits at the smallest infringement or misstep.

"Any trouble last night?" Habakkuk asked Chuwl. "I have heard rumors of other shepherds having trouble with jackals of late."

"No trouble, Master," Chuwl replied through a mouthful of cheese and bread. "But two nights past we killed two of the beasts. They were more aggressive than usual."

"Bad sign," another shepherd said, and the others grunted their agreement.

"But, no sheep were injured," Chuwl continued. "They hardly knew what was going on."

A team of shepherds never all slept at the same time. At least one stayed awake—even through the darkest and quietest times of night—to keep watch for attacking jackals or wolves. Habakkuk knew his men would risk their lives for the flock and often had. For, indeed, their own livelihood depended on the well-being of the animals they kept.

If, in the unlikely event a sheep or goat were wounded or became ill, the men used their expert knowledge of medicinal herbs to quickly treat the ailing animal. Shepherds, in general, were often so good at this that, if a physician or midwife could not be found in town, a shepherd was considered the next best alternative. Shepherds also displayed an uncanny ability to find water—even in the most arid places—as if they could smell it.

Chuwl finished his mouthful and stood up. Walking a few paces from the group of men, he faced the flock and let out a shrill whistle, drawing the animals' attention. He lifted his arms and made wide sweeping motions above his head. Habakkuk watched in admiration as a few of the sheep began to move, and then several more, and then more. Slowly, the entire flock became aware of the shift and moved to the far side of the narrow valley, where the grass was more plentiful. The dogs followed the herd and resumed their guard.

Each time Chuwl did this Habakkuk was amazed, for certainly sheep were the dumbest and most wayward animals of all Elohim's created beings. But, the longer a shepherd stayed with the flock, the more manageable the flock became. They learned his voice and became peaceful and gentle at his approach.

Habakkuk stood, smiling and shaking his head in admiration.

"I am going for a short stroll. Help yourselves to whatever is left of the food," he said, motioning to the meal spread out on a white linen cloth on a rock.

Habakkuk walked along a sloping hillside alone. From where he stood, he could still see the animals meandering about the valley. Last spring had been a very profitable one in which many new lambs had been born. Several of the ewes had even birthed twins. Now his flock had nearly grown to the size it had been before Pharaoh exacted his heavy tribute. Their fleece was thick and healthy. Fall would soon be upon them, and then it would be time for the second shearing.

The shepherds would lead the sheep into a pool where each animal would be scrubbed and washed to remove the dirt, burs, and vermin from their wool. Then the men would wait for it to dry again before beginning the arduous task of shearing. Tiph'arah and his daughters would take the wool and again wash it and then comb it. Some of the fleece would be divided among the shepherds or spun and woven into new clothing. Each year, the shepherds received a new tunic from Tiph'arah and, every three years, she made them new cloaks. Whatever remained of the fleece was traded for other goods.

The flocks provided many other goods as well. The goat hair could be made into garment cloth, tent coverings, and even pillows. The female sheep and goats that had given birth were also milked regularly. This provided not only milk, but cheese and butter. Sour goat milk could be turned into *leben*, a favorite yogurt-like dish. When butchered, sheep provided meat, and Habakkuk's family used the skins to make bags, coverings, sandals, and drum tops. Goat hide was turned into wineskins. Whatever they did not use for themselves would be sold at the market, and part of the profit was divided among the shepherds.

Habakkuk sighed with satisfaction. If things continued this way, by next spring he would be back to his former level of prosperity, and he could easily cover the expense of Zamiyr's wedding. As he thought these things, he felt a very strong, hot wind rise up behind him and blow roughly past him toward the valley.

The wind grew steadily in intensity. It rushed past his ears and moved through his hair and beard. The heat felt surprisingly strong for this time of the year. He had left his cloak in the valley and so had no protection from the blast.

Habakkuk rubbed the back of his neck in discomfort and blinked his eyes against the draft. He looked again toward the valley and saw, to his horror that, as the scorching wind passed by him and reached the grasses, the greenery immediately began to turn brown and wither. As the gentle breeze had formerly played in the grass, it now brought death with its touch. The curling, blazing wind passed over the earth in a wave of devastation, exposing the uneven earth and rocks as it went. Habakkuk watched helplessly as the burning wind encroached on his flock. It came upon them, withering the very grass in their mouths. They, too, began to wither and thin and die beneath its force.

Strangely, the shepherds saw nothing. They remained under the oak tree—from which leaves fell like rain upon and around them—enjoying their jokes and their wine. How could they not see what he saw? Why did they not rise and get the flock to shelter?

The back of his neck, his arms, and calves now burned, and the wind stung his eyes. He rubbed at his eyes fiercely but, when he opened them again, the scene before him had changed. The grasses were again green. The sheep still grazed lazily in the valley, and the oak tree still provided shade for his laughing shepherds.

Habakkuk took a deep breath and swallowed hard against the intense beating of his heart. He touched the back of his neck again and the pain was gone. A cool, gentle breeze blew refreshingly against his skin and his eyes no longer watered. But even though all seemed well, Habakkuk knew

Elohim had sent him a message. He knelt there and prayed in fervent supplication.

Adonai! Please spare us from this drought you are sending on the land! Why are we being punished, Adonai?

Even as Habakkuk said these words, his mind returned to what he had seen that very morning—his neighbor, Pinon, praying and cutting himself before one of the Canaanite's detestable gods.

Forgive us, Adonai, for our evil ways and teach us to follow You with our whole hearts! Rid us of idolatry and wickedness!

But even though Habakkuk prayed and pleaded for the rest of the afternoon, he knew Elohim's warning was not to be taken lightly. A drought would come, and Elohim had sent a vision of warning to His prophet. Now, Habakkuk must warn the people.

✡   ✡   ✡

"What are we to do?" Zemor asked nervously after hearing Habakkuk's warning at the men's evening circle that night. "Is there time to save and prepare?"

"We should not panic!" Nebelah said with irritation. "Who is to say one man's dream is worth sending the entire valley into an uproar?"

"He was right about Sebat," Mishmereth said loyally, knowing his words would touch a tender spot. "You, of all people, should not doubt the nabiy's word."

"So we are to just sit by and let our land be cursed by this sorcerer?" he raged, recalling his former wrath. "His God is bent on our destruction!"

"No, no!" Cheresh said, trying to calm the assembly of worried men. "The great LORD Elohim is good! He does not wish for us to perish! If He did, why warn us at all?"

"Why curse us at all?" Nebelah hurled back. "A good God would not do such a thing! Let us call on Osiris, god of rebirth, fertility, and agriculture, to save us!"

This suggestion triggered an uproar of angry shouts and accusations.

"He is also the god of death and the underworld, you fool! He may just as soon kill us all!"

"How could you even say such a thing after all Josiah did to rid us of foreign religions?"

"Egypt is a fickle friend! They promise protection and deliverance but, when the battle begins, where are they? Again and again they have failed to come to our aid!"

"How dare you suggest we honor the gods of Egypt, after what the Egyptians have done to our nation?"

Nebelah raised his hands and scrambled to reply to the onslaught. He finally made himself heard, "That is precisely why we should seek protection from the gods of Egypt! Do you not see? Egypt sees us as part of their land—their people! Their gods will see us the same way. Regardless of how the Egyptians treat us, why should we not seek protection from their gods? They might be very favorable to us and bless us greatly in the future for our unexpected obedience and reverence! And, if you would prefer to seek protection of a different god, perhaps Ipet, goddess of magical protection, could be persuaded to shield us from Habakkuk's curses!"

"But how are we to be sure she would help us?" another asked.

"What if it just makes Elohim angrier with us?" Zemor asked, his tone suggesting he was considering Nebelah's suggestion.

"What kind of ceremonies does Ipet require?" yet another asked.

Habakkuk felt rage rising within his chest as he heard his friends and neighbors speaking such obvious blasphemy. But suddenly, he saw Zanah's dark figure again, moving about the edges of the crowd like a slithering serpent as she had on a previous night. She looked up. Her eyes met his with an immediate, piercing gaze. If her eyes had been any less intense, they would have been lost in the wild maze of black tattoos. But she looked right at him and, even through the black lines and designs masking her features, he recognized a look of triumph.

She turned away, but the feeling in his gut changed from anger to helpless frustration. He stood, drawing the stares of many of the men, who still debated about how they might magically avoid the coming drought. Their conversations ceased as they saw him stride to the center of the courtyard, fire in his eyes.

"Do as you will!" Habakkuk shouted. "I came to give you warning as Elohim instructed, but I came with reluctance, wondering why He would allow this hardship. Now I see why! You call yourselves sons of Abraham and you pretend to honor Elohim with your sacrifices and your false words of worship, but see how quickly you seek after idols and false gods! Elohim is right to test us in this way! You have deserted Him in your hearts! You crave evil and lust after the obscene gods of the Egyptians and Canaanites! But do not be deceived! If that is what you long for, you will have it! Elohim will give you what you seek! ...But not what you expect!"

He turned and left them mumbling and fretting amongst themselves. Habakkuk did not go directly home. Far too angry and broken inside to step into the midst of his family, he walked the city roads through the growing darkness, trudging his anger into the ground.

✡ ✡ ✡

The sheep shearing went well, and Habakkuk's family and servants carefully collected and laundered the wool. Habakkuk traded the extra for large quantities of grain, which he sealed with mud into three large clay jars. He placed his personal seal on the lid and, when it had dried, he buried them in the ground under their house. Over the next couple of months they were able to do the same with two kegs of wine, one keg of beer, and a jar of lentils. Tiph'arah and the girls went into the hills to gather as many herbs as they could find and dried them next to the fire. Then they sealed them into jars and buried them, as well. Zimrah gathered olives from their tree, and Yadah crushed them to oil on their small olive press in the courtyard, complaining it made her shoulders and back sore.

With all the extra work, Habakkuk had no time to make or sell instruments, so Shachar took over those duties and spent many hours on the roof fashioning lyres or flutes. He also proved to be a very persuasive salesman with his open smile and ease with strangers. Habakkuk was impressed and relieved for, although he enjoyed fashioning instruments and greatly enjoyed playing them, it was not in his nature to relish the sales portion of the business.

News of the coming drought spread quickly throughout Judah, though reactions varied. Those who knew and trusted Habakkuk began planning and saving for the coming year. But most dismissed it as another of many false prophesies of doom that had met their ears over the decades from various self-proclaimed oracles and soothsayers.

To add to the confusion, other prophets arrived in town and stood in the shuk and at the city gates proclaiming with equal force that no drought would come. Enchanters and diviners offered their services—for a good price—to call out to Ipet or Ishtar or Ba'al for protection. Instead of saving and preparing, many of the People spent what extra they had making sacrifices and paying diviners to perform magical ceremonies on their behalf. They worshipped on hilltops and copulated wildly in the fields and under every spreading tree in an attempt to ensure fertility to the land. Habakkuk began to wonder if his warning had done more evil than good.

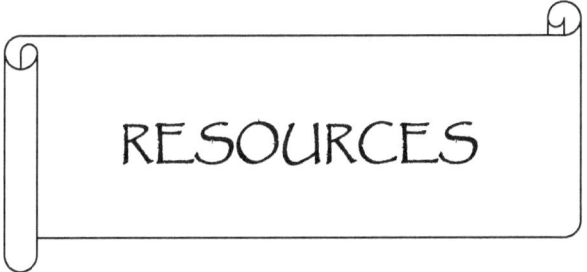

People, Places, and Things

Abba   Hebrew word for father, dad, or daddy.

Adonai   ('Ădônây) Adonai is the transliterated Hebrew word for "Lord," signifying majesty and sovereignty.

Ailsa   Fictional mother of Habakkuk. Tribe of Levi. Transliterated Hebrew word meaning: consecrated to God.

Anath   Canaanite goddess of fertility.

Apsu   Babylonian god and head of the pantheon. His consort is Tiamat. He represented fresh waters, while she represented salt seas.

Arad   Arad was a city to the southeast of Jerusalem in the Negev region.

Asherah   Asherah (also called Athirat & Elat) was one of the several fertility goddesses of the Canaanite people. The Asherah pole was used in combination with an altar in their fertility rites and ceremonies. Sometimes a naturally growing terebinth tree was used instead of a pole fashioned by hand, and these sites were most often located on hilltops (high places).

Ashtoreth   Canaanite fertility goddess (pl: Ashtaroth; used to refer to idols) worshipped along the seacoast. Baal was her male consort. Worship rites involved lewd sexual practices.

Asshur   Assyrian city on the Tigris River. It was at one time the capital.

Assurbanipal   Assurbanipal (Ashurbanipal), son of Esar-haddon, was the Assyrian ruler from 669 B.C.E. until 633 B.C.E.

Assur-uballit II   King of Haran during Assyrian rule.

Assyrians   A people group who dominated the Near East for over three centuries. They were known for their idolatry, brutality, and tyrannical methods. In 722 B.C.E. the fall of Samaria to the Assyrian king, Tiglath-pilesar III, marked the end of the northern kingdom of Israel. The people were murdered or exiled, and the area was resettled by Assyrians, who intermarried with what remained of the Hebrew people living there, thus instilling hatred between the full-blooded Jews from the south and the "half-breed" Samaritans of the north.

Azariah

Dates, names and succession of high priests are historically unclear. However, based on the available information, Azariah is the most likely candidate to have fulfilled the role of High Priest during this era.

Ba'al

Ba'al (or Baal), meaning "lord", was the Canaanite god of thunder and fertility (including agriculture, animal husbandry and human sexuality). Worship practices often involved lewd, sexual acts.

Babylon

Capital city of the Babylonian empire. Located on the Euphrates River in the Fertile Crescent, with the river flowing through it. Under Nebuchadnezzar II, it became a city of luxury and fame.

Babylonians

The Neo-Babylonian Empire (614-539 B.C.E.) was begun by Nabopolassar, a Chaldean prince, by defeating Assyria with the aid of Media.

Beersheba

Beersheba was a city in the Negev that designated the southern end of Judah.

Bethel

A town located twelve miles north of Jerusalem and mentioned often in Scripture. Abraham offered a sacrifice here on his way to the Negev; Jacob's dream of the ladder reaching to Heaven occurred here; the ark was kept here during the period of the judges; it became a place of idolatry until Josiah's reformation.

Bitumen

Asphalt in its natural state, pitch, tar. Used as mortar.

Bull of Heaven

The Bull of Heaven was the vicious beast against which Gilgamesh and Enkidu did battle in the 12-tablet Babylonian epic about Gilgamesh's search for immortality.

Calendar

Hebrew	Babylonian	Modern
Nisan (Abib)	Nisanu	Mar./Apr.
Iyyar	Ayaru	Apr./May
Sivan	Siwanu/Simanu	May/June
Tammuz	Du'uzu	June/July
Ab	Abu	July/Aug.
Elul	Elulu/Ululu	Aug./Sept.
Tishri	Tisritu	Sept./Oct.
(Mar)hesvan	(W)arah-sammu	Oct./Nov.
Kislev	Kisliwu/Kislimu	Nov./Dec.
Tebet	Tebitu	Dec./Jan.
Shebat	Sabatu	Jan./Feb.
Adar	Addaru	Feb./Mar.

Caphar

Fictional father of Me'ah, man accidentally killed by Shachar. Transliterated Hebrew word meaning: to count, recount, relate.

Canaanite

Canaanite territory had often undefined borders; however, it generally occupied the Palestinian territory west of the Jordan River, portions of southern Syria to the north and portions of the Negev region to the south. The Canaanite people were polytheistic.

Chaldeans

The Chaldeans were a mixture of tribes that shared Mesopotamia. The peoples were largely Babylonian inhabitants, Sumerians and Akkadians.

Challamiysh

Fictional grandfather of Shachar. Transliterated Hebrew word meaning: hardness, flint, rock.

Chayil

Fictional brother-in-law of Habakkuk. Transliterated Hebrew word meaning: strength, might, efficiency, wealth, army (valiant).

Chemdah

Fictional sister of Habakkuk. Transliterated Hebrew word meaning: precious, desirable.

Chemosh	Chemosh was the national god of Moab (but was also associated with the Ammonites). He was the god of war and demanded child sacrifice.
Chen	Fictional niece of Habakkuk, third child of Chemdah. Transliterated Hebrew word meaning: favor, grace, charm.
Cheresh	Fictional local priest in Hebron. Transliterated Hebrew word meaning: silently, secretly, magic art, magician.
City of Refuge	Six cities of refuge were set apart by Moses and Joshua: Bezer, Ramoth Gilead, Golan, Hebron, Shechem, and Kedesh. These cities provided asylum only for those who took a life by accident. They were positioned so that one could travel in no more than one day to a city of refuge from any part of Palestine. See: Numbers 35, Deuteronomy 19:1-13, and Joshua 20. A refugee, if found innocent of willful murder, was allowed to remain unharmed within the city until the death of the high priest. Then he would be allowed to return home, unharmed; however, if he was discovered outside the city, the blood avenger had the right to his life.
Dagon	Principle god of the Philistines, but worshipped throughout Mesopotamia.
Dara	In "Hadarah's Story," Dara is Hadarah's fictional mother. Her name means 'mercy.'
David	King David, often referred to as "Israel's Beloved Singer", was the second king of Israel, before the division of the kingdom. He is the most famous and most loved of all the Hebrew kings and it was prophesied the Messiah would be born of his genealogical line.
Day of Atonement	See: Yom Kippur.
Egypt	Located on the Nile River in Northern Africa. Notoriously untrustworthy as allies to the Hebrew people, they continue to remain symbolic of their captivity and rescue from slavery by God via Moses.

El	El is an ancient Semitic word meaning "deity", perhaps "power". Poetically used by the Hebrews for the true God of Israel, but the word was also used by the Canaanites to denote the senior god of their pantheon.
El Shaddai	('êl Shadday) El Shaddai is Hebrew for "God Almighty".
Elam	Elam was located in southwest Asia, east of Babylonia and north of the Persian Gulf (now modern southwest Iran). The Elamites were a mixture of dark-skinned aboriginals and Semites who lived in constant strife with Sumerians, Babylonians, Assyrians and, later, the Persians.
Elasah	In "Hadarah's Story," Elasah is Hadarah's fictional father. Elasah means 'God has wrought.'
Eliakim	See: Jehoiakim.
Eloah	('êlôahh) Eloah is the Hebrew name for God meaning, He alone is worthy of worship.
Elohim	('ĕlôhîym) A Hebrew word for the supreme God. He is the great Creator God of the Hebrews, supreme and plural of majesty.
Enkidu	Best friend of Gilgamesh in the 12-tablet Babylonian epic tale.
Gath	One of five primary Philistine cities on southern coast of Palestine.
Gaza	A city on the coast of the Mediterranean Sea about 50 miles W, SW of Jerusalem, formerly under the control of the Philistines.
Gedaliah	Governor of Judah after the Babylonian conquest of 586 B.C.E. He was assassinated after only two or three months by Jewish nationalists under the leadership of Ishmael. His death instigated mass Jewish flight to Egypt, leaving Judah without a significant Jewish presence until after the return from Exile.
Gilgamesh	Hero of a 12-tablet Babylonian epic tale.

Habakkuk	One of the Old Testament minor prophets. His name means: "one who embraces" or "one who clings". The name itself is not Hebrew in origin. Scholars believe it comes from an Assyrian root word.
Hadarah	Fictional grandmother of Habakkuk. Her name meaning, 'beauty.'
Hamath	Name of both a city and a region 125 miles north of Damascus on the Orontes River.
Hamutal	One of Josiah's wives, of Libnah. Mother of Shallum (Jehoahaz).
Haran	(Or, Harran) A Mesopotamian city located on a strategic trade route that became a major Assyrian stronghold. It was besieged and conquered by Nabopolassar in 610 B.C.E. By 609 it had become a part of the Neo-Babylonian Empire.
Hebron	A city 25 miles south/southwest of Jerusalem. It is located in fertile foothills, south of which lies the Negev.
Hilkiah	High Priest during the reign of Josiah at the time the Temple was repaired and the Book of the Law was found. Azariah was his son.
Imah	Hebrew word for "mom" or "mommy."
Ishtar	(Also, Inanna or "queen of heaven") Principle goddess of the Mesopotamian pantheon and consort of Dumuzi. She evidences a duality of nature in being associated with love, war, fertility, sexuality, passion, and anger. Worship rites included a sacred marriage ritual between the king and a priestess in order to ensure successful crops for the coming year.
Israel	Name of united kingdom under David and Solomon and then of the Northern Kingdom after the divide. Its capital was Samaria.
Ivah	Fictional father of Shachar, originally from Lachish. Hebrew word meaning: perverter.

Jared	In "Hadarah's Story: Part I," Jared is the fictional boy Hadarah becomes betrothed to. His name means 'a descender.'
Jehoahaz	Fourth son of Josiah by Hamutal, seventeenth king of Judah. Name means "Jehovah seized".
Jehoiachin	Son of Jehoiakim who succeeded his father to the throne of Judah and reigned for only three months before being taken into captivity when Nebuchadnezzar marched on Judah.
Jehoiakim	Second son of Josiah by Zebudah, eighteenth king of Judah. Name means "Jehovah will establish."
Jeriel	Fictional father of Habakkuk. Hebrew word meaning: May God teach.
Jerusalem	Capital city of Israel, before divide, and of Judah after the kingdom divided into Israel in the north and Judah in the south. Home of the City of David and Solomon's Temple.
Josiah	King Josiah, son of evil King Amon, was the sixteenth king of the southern kingdom of Judah. He ruled from 640 B.C.E. until 609 B.C.E.
Judah	Name of the Southern Kingdom after the divided monarchy. Named for the tribe of Judah. Jerusalem remained their capital.
Juttah	A Levitical city in the hill country of Judah.
Kethem	Fictional nephew of Habakkuk, sixth child of Yashab. Transliterated Hebrew word meaning: gold, pure gold.
Kothar-wa-Khasis	Canaanite deity worshipped as a master craftsman, a soothsayer, and a caster of magical spells.
Lachish	Lachish was a walled city to the southwest of Jerusalem. It was destroyed in a notorious battle with the Assyrians in 701 B.C., but was later rebuilt.

Levite	A Levite was a member of the tribe of Levi. The men of this tribe were set apart to be responsible for service in and around the temple. This was their reward for remaining faithful to God when the others worshipped the golden calf at Mt. Horeb in Exodus 32.
Libnah	City in Judah.
Lute	Musical instrument, not unlike a guitar. Stings stretched over a neck and a hollow box are plucked or strummed to make music.
Lyre	Harp-like stringed musical instrument.
Machmad	Fictional nephew of Habakkuk, oldest child of Yashab. Transliterated Hebrew word meaning: precious treasures, desirable thing, pleasant thing.
Manasseh	King Manasseh was the grandfather of King Josiah and the thirteenth king of Judah. He reigned for 55-years, from 696 to 642 B.C.E.
Mar'eh	Fictional niece of Habakkuk, fourth child of Yashab. Transliterated Hebrew word meaning: a view, seeing, appearance, whether, comeliness, fair countenance, beautiful.
Mattanah	Fictional nephew of Habakkuk, first child of Chemdah. Transliterated Hebrew word meaning: gift.
Me'ah	Fictional character. Man accidentally killed by Shachar. Transliterated Hebrew word meaning: offspring.
Media	Media was the region of modern northwest Iran. They inhabited a defined area of the Zagros Mountains and were closely related to the Persians. They were instrumental in the final defeat of the Assyrians.
Megiddo	An ancient city located in the southwestern portion of the Jezreel Valley. It lies along a major pass connecting Egypt with Syria and Mesopotamia.
Metheq	Fictional nephew of Habakkuk, second child of Yashab. Transliterated Hebrew word meaning: sweetness.

Mishmereth   Fictional friend of Habakkuk, a watchtower guard of Hebron. Transliterated Hebrew word meaning: watch, sentry, the post.

Molech   Molech (literally translated as "king") was the detestable god of the Ammonites. He was also called Milcom or Malcham. Worship of this god often involved human sacrifices.

Mot   Canaanite god of death.

Nabiy   Hebrew word for "prophet".

Nabopolassar   First king of the Neo-Babylonian Empire (625-605 B.C.E.) and father of Nebuchadnezzar II. He died while his son was fighting the Battle of Carchemish against Pharaoh Nekau II of Egypt.

Nabu   Babylonian god of wisdom and writing and the herald of the gods.

Nahum   A biblical prophet and contemporary of Habakkuk. He prophesied during the latter half of the seventh century B.C., writing the biblical book that bears his name sometime around 630 B.C.

Name   "The Name" was how traditional Jews often referred to God. In reverence, they refrained from speaking His true name (YHWH) except once a year on the Day of Atonement when the High Priest would speak it at the Temple.

Na'veh   Fictional mother of Shachar. Transliterated Hebrew word meaning: comely, beautiful, seemly.

Nebelah   Fictional Hebron elder. Transliterated Hebrew word meaning: flabby thing, dead thing, dead idol.

Nebuchadnezzar II   Son of the Chaldean king of the Neo-Babylonian Empire, Nabopolassar, who succeeded his father to the throne. He became famous for his massive, elaborate building projects (including the Ishtar Gate and the Hanging Gardens), military might and great wealth and influence.

Negev   The Negev (Negeb) is a vast area of dry land in southern Judah, used primarily as pasturelands.

Nekau II   Pharaoh Nekau II (Neco, Necho, Nechoh) of Egypt, son of Psamtik I (Psammetichus), reigned from 610 B.C. until 595 B.C.E.

Nevi'im   Nevi'im is the second main division of the Hebrew Bible, between the Torah and Ketuvim. It contains two sub-groups, the Former Prophets and the Latter Prophets.

Nimrud   (Also, Calah) City in Assyria.

Nineveh   City on the Tigris River and long-time capital of the Assyrian Empire.

Pantheon   The set of gods belonging to a particular religion, mythology or tradition.

Passover   Most important Jewish holiday celebrated to remember how God delivered them from Egyptian slavery through the ten plagues, which culminated in the death of the first born son. By following specific directions from God, the Angel of Death "passed over" their first born sons and they were spared from death. This last plague convinced Pharaoh to let the Hebrew slaves go free.

Philistia   Region on the southern coast of Palestine, home of the Philistine peoples.

Raphad   Fictional Egyptian manservant of Habakkuk. Hebrew transliterated word meaning: refresh.

Ranan   Fictional nephew of Habakkuk, seventh child of Yashab, twin of Samach. Transliterated Hebrew word meaning: joyfully singing, shout for joy.

Reuben   In "Hadarah's Story," Reuben is the fictional father of Jared, the boy Hadarah becomes betrothed to. His name means 'see ye, a son.'

Riblah	A city on the east bank of the Orantes River north of Damascus in Assyrian territory.
Rinnah	Fictional second child (female) of Habakkuk. Transliterated Hebrew word meaning: joyful singing, joyful shouting
Rumah	A city in Israel to the north of Judah and dominated by the Assyrians.
Sakal	Fictional older brother of Shachar. Transliterated Hebrew word meaning: intelligence, consider, expert, prudent, skillful, successful.
Samach	Fictional nephew of Habakkuk, eighth child of Yashab, twin of Ranan. Transliterated Hebrew word meaning: give them joy.
Samaria	Capital of the Northern Kingdom of Israel during the days of the Divided Kingdom. It was occupied by the Assyrians at the time of this story.
Scythians	A people who lived north of the Black Sea, known for their advanced cavalry.
Sebat	Fictional man of Hebron; friend of Nebelah; husband of Tuwb. Hebrew word meaning: smite thou.
Sennacherib	Assyrian king and son of Sargon II who reigned from 704-681 B.C.E. and invaded Judah during the reign of King Hezekiah.
Shachar	Fictional refugee. Transliterated Hebrew word meaning: diligently seek. An association between this name and Sahar exists. Sahar is the Canaanite god of the dawn.
Shalom	Traditional Hebrew greeting, meaning: Peace.
Shallum	See: Jehoahaz.
Shamar	Fictional friend of Habakkuk, watchtower guard of Hebron. Transliterated Hebrew word meaning: guard, protect.

Shemesh	(Or Shamash) Sun god and god of law and justice. He was widely worshipped in Canaanite, Assyrian, and Babylonian religious tradition.
Shiloh	Ancient holy site 17 miles north of Bethel where the tent of meeting and the ark of the covenant was once kept but was destroyed (the method is historically unclear) and became a ruin by the time of Jeremiah's ministry.
Shuk	The marketplace: a place of commerce that dominated city life, both in business, in personal transactions, and in the spreading of local, regional and national news.
Siyach	Fictional nephew of Habakkuk, second child of Chemdah. Transliterated Hebrew word meaning: put forth, mediate, muse, commune, speak, complain, ponder, sing.
Solomon	King Solomon, son of King David and Bathsheba, was the third king of Israel and the last full reign before the nation split into the northern (Israel) and southern (Judah) kingdoms. He reigned 40 years, from 970 to 930 B.C.E. He was renowned for his wisdom and God blessed him also with great riches, peace and a long life. (I Kings 1:28-11:43 & 2 Chronicles 1-9)
Syria	Not to be confused with Assyria, Syria is a region extending from the eastern border of the Mediterranean Sea northward toward the Euphrates River in the northwest, the Taurus Mountains in the northeast, and southward, sometimes including Palestine and Phoenicia.
Tam	Fictional niece of Habakkuk, third child of Yashab. Transliterated Hebrew word meaning: peace.
Tanah	Fictional sister-in-law of Habakkuk, wife of Yashab. Transliterated Hebrew word meaning: to recount, rehearse, tell again.
Teraph	(Teraphim, plural.) Small, household idols and pagan objects of worship. Referred to as "disgraceful things" in rabbinical literature.

Terebinth tree	The terebinth tree is a large, deciduous tree common to the area. It is often associated with pagan religious practices.
Tiamat	Babylonian goddess of the sea and chaos.
Tikrit	Mesopotamian city located on the Tigris River.
Timbrel	A musical instrument, such as a small hand drum. It possibly also bore small bells or clinking pieces of metal.
Tiph'arah	Fictional wife of Habakkuk. Transliterated Hebrew word meaning: beauty, bravery, comely, glory, honor, majesty.
Topheth	A place in the Valley of Hinnom meaning "place of burning" where worshippers burned their children alive to the god Molech.
Tuwb	Fictional character; wife of Sebat of Hebron. Transliterated Hebrew word meaning: goodness.
Valley of Hinnom	(Also, Gehenna) A valley located just south of the city of Jerusalem. Due to the detestable practices of pagan idolaters, who sacrificed their children to the Canaanite god Molech in this valley, the word has become synonymous with Hell.
Yadah	Fictional third child (female) of Habakkuk. Transliterated Hebrew word meaning: giving praise.
Yagrush and Ayamur	According to the myths of Ba'al, they are legendary, magical clubs created by Kothar-wa-Khasis for Ba'al. Ba'al used them to defeat Yam.
Yashab	Fictional older brother of Habakkuk. Transliterated Hebrew word meaning: peaceful.
Yam	Deity worshipped in Canaan as god of the sea and the primordial chaos.
Yediyd	Fictional niece of Habakkuk, fifth child of Yashab. Transliterated Hebrew word meaning: beloved.

Yom Kippur	Yom Kippur is the transliterated Hebrew word meaning: Day of Atonement. It is often referred to as simply "The Day". It is the holiest and most solemn of the Jewish holy days and is commemorated by fasting and attending synagogue services. It is time to reflect on oneself, repent for wrongdoing and right oneself with God.
Zamiyr	Fictional first child (female) of Habakkuk. Transliterated Hebrew word meaning: song, psalm.
Zaham	Fictional man who Habakkuk rescues from bandits on the road between Jerusalem and Hebron. Name means: he loathed.
Zanah	Fictional pagan witch of Hebron. Transliterated Hebrew word meaning: unfaithful harlot.
Zaqen	Fictional lame, old basket-weaver and friend of Habakkuk. Transliterated Hebrew word meaning: to be old, become old.
Zephaniah	A biblical prophet and contemporary of Habakkuk. He was the great, great grandson of Hezekiah and prophesied in Jerusalem His ministry roughly spanned King Josiah's reign, 640-609 B.C.
Zebudah	Wife of King Josiah, from Rumah, and mother of Jehoiakim.
Zemor	Fictional character. Wealthy vineyard owner of Hebron. Transliterated Hebrew word meaning: twig, vine, branch.
Zimrah	Fictional fourth child (female) of Habakkuk. Transliterated Hebrew word meaning: song.

Scripture References

Hadarah's Story　　The short story opens with Elasah quoting Genesis 12:1-4a.

Chapter Two　　"I lift up my eyes to the hills—where does my help come from? My help comes from the LORD, the Maker of heaven and earth. He will not let your foot slip—he who watches over you will not slumber; indeed, *he who watches over Israel will neither slumber nor sleep.* The LORD watches over you-- the LORD is your shade at your right hand; the sun will not harm you by day, nor the moon by night. The LORD will keep you from all harm—he will watch over your life; the LORD will watch over your coming and going both now and forevermore." Psalm 121:1-8 (emphasis added)

"A perverse man stirs up dissension, and a gossip separates close friends." Proverbs 16:28

Chapter Three　　Whirlwind Curse: See Hosea 8:7

Chapter Five　　Last, poetic passage is taken from Psalm 8.

Chapter Seven　　Prophet Zephaniah is quoted where he predicts that the Assyrian city, Nineveh, will be left "utterly desolate and as dry as the desert." This was a particularly significant prophesy, given that the city would become known for its vast, lush gardens and parks. See Zephaniah 2:13-15 for this prophet's words against Assyria and Nineveh. Also, see the book of Nahum for that prophet's energetic prophesies of doom to Nineveh. The actual destruction of the city occurred in 612 B.C. It was then abandoned and forgotten until it was rediscovered by archeologists in 1845.

Chapter Nine　　"So, when Elohim tells us to love Him with all our heart and with all our soul and with all our strength, He really means all of it—not just part." Explanation of Deuteronomy 6:5.

Chapter Fourteen   Story of the return of the Ark of the Covenant can
be found in I Samuel 8.

Works Consulted

Backhouse, Robert. The Kregel Pictorial Guide to The Temple. Grand Rapids, MI: Kregel Publications, 1996.

Baker, Waren, D.R.E., ed. The Complete Word Study Old Testament, KJV. Chattanooga: AMG Publishers, 1994.

Bible History Online, www.bible-history.com

Boadt, Lawrence. Reading the Old Testament: An Introduction. New York: Paulist Press, 1984.

Bottero, Jean. Antonia Nevill, translator. Everyday Life in Ancient Mesopotamia. Baltimore, Maryland: Johns Hopkins University Press, 2001.

Bright, John. A History of Israel, 3rd Edition. Philadelphia: Westminster Press, 1981.

Chiera, Edward. They Wrote on Clay. Chicago: The University of Chicago Press, 1938.

Contenau, Georges. Everyday Life in Babylon and Assyria. New York: W.W. Norton & Company, Inc., 1966.

Dowley, Tim. The Kregel Pictorial Guide to Everyday Life in Bible Times. Grand Rapids, MI: Kregel Publications, 1999.

Elwell, Walter A. Baker Encyclopedia of the Bible, Volumes 1 & 2. Grand Rapids, Michigan: Baker Book House, 1988.

Finkelstein, Israel and Neil Asher Silberman. The Bible Unearthed: Archaeology's New Vision of Ancient Israel and The Origin of Its Sacred Texts. New York: The Free Press, 2001.

Frank, Harry Thomas, ed. Atlas of the Bible Lands. Revised Edition. Hammond Inc., 2002.

Freedman, David Noel, ed. Eerdman's Dictionary of the Bible. Grand Rapids, MI: Wm. B. Eerdman's Publishing Company, 2000.

Grosvenor, Melville Bell and Frederick G. Vosburgh, eds. Everyday Life in Bible Times. National Geographic Society, 1967.

Honour, Alan. Treasures Under the Sand: Woolley's Finds at Ur. New York: McGraw-Hill Book Company, 1967.

Howard, Kevin and Marvin Rosenthal. The Feasts of the Lord. Nashville, TN: Thomas Nelson, Inc., 1997.

McNeill, William H. and Jean W. Sedlar. The Origins of Civilization. New York: Oxford University Press, 1968.

Packer, J.I., and M.C. Tenney, eds. Illustrated Manners and Customs of the Bible. Nashville: Thomas Nelson Publishers, 1980.

Pearlman, Moshe. Digging Up the Bible: The Stories Behind the Great Archaeological Discoveries in the Holy Land. New York: William Morrow and Company, Inc., 1980.

Pritchard, James B., ed. The Ancient Near East: An Anthology of Texts and Pictures. Princeton University Press, 1958.

Pritchard, James B. ed. The Ancient Near East, Volume II: A New Anthology of Texts and Pictures. Princeton University Press, 1975.

Roux, Georges. Ancient Iraq. London: Penguin Books, 1992.

Telushkin, Rabbi Joseph. Jewish Literacy: The Most Important Things To Know About the Jewish Religion, Its People and Its History. New York: William Morrow and Company, Inc., 2001.

Vamosh, Miriam Feinberg. Food at the Time of the Bible: From Adam's Apple to the Last Supper. Abingdon Press, 2004.

Vos, Howard F. Nelson's New Illustrated Bible Manners and Customs. Nashville, TN: Thomas Nelson, Inc., 1999.

Walvoord, John F. and Roy B. Zuck. The Bible Knowledge Commentary: Old Testament. Victor Books, 1983.

Whiston, William, A. M., translator. The Works of Josephus. Hendrickson Publishers, 1987.

Wood, Leon J. A Survey of Israel's History. Grand Rapids, MI: Zondervan Publishing House, 1970.

Wright, Ernest G., ed. Great People of the Bible and How They Lived. Reader's Digest Association, Inc., 1971.

Wright, Paul H. Holman QuickSource Guide: Atlas of Bible Lands. Nashville, TN: Holman Bible Publishers, 2002.

More From:

@TDPPress
www.TheDramaticPen.com
Facebook.com/TheDramaticPen

The Scrolls of the Nevi'im Series Continues with:

**Book II
Habakkuk's Plea:
Evil Persists**

**Book III
Habakkuk's Plea:
Elohim Answers**

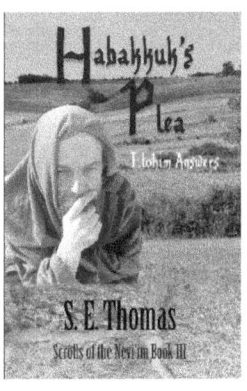

Longing for Rest
A Novella
By S. E. Thomas

One heartbroken woman battles insomnia. Another cannot escape the coma trapping her between dreams and reality. Though they have never met, through a miraculous crossing of consciousness, they find themselves together on a grassy hill surrounded by a mysterious fog. In this dream world, Amy and Gracie form an unusual friendship. But will fear, pain, and betrayal follow them and spoil this haven? Will they finally be able to rest? Can a dream change your life? Available in paperback ($7.99) or eBook ($2.99 from Kindle or Nook.)

The Sixth Hour
Book I of the Holy Land Mysteries Series
By S. E. Thomas

Can Darash, a Jewish teenager, track a killer, rescue his family from ruin, and discover the truth about Yeshua? The rebel, Yeshua, drove the merchants and moneychangers from the Temple with a whip. Hours later, one of them was murdered. Now fifteen-year-old Darash must find a way to protect his family from poverty even as he struggles with the grief of losing his father. When another murder is committed, Darash finds himself searching for a dangerous killer and relying on an old, blind basket-weaver for help. Despite the odds, Darash discovers he has strength of character, a deep compassion for others, and an uncanny knack for problem-solving. But will he be able to expose the killer before the killer finds him?

The Holy Land Mysteries Series
Darash's adventures continue with…
Book II: The Brazen Altar
Book III: The Mud Flower
Book IV: The Leper's Gift
Book V: The Weeping Place
And More!

Be Inspired by Poetry from Montana Artists of All Ages

Into the Beautiful
Poetry by Montana Artists
Volume One

"Into the Beautiful: Poetry by Montana Artists" (Vol.1, 2015) is a collection of poetry by Montana artists of all ages. These works of art and creativity were collected through annual contests run August through October. To find out more about this contest, please visit our website at TheDramaticPen.com.

Throw a Mystery Party!
Who Invited The Stiff to Dinner?
A Mystery Party Game for Teens and Adults
By S. E. Thomas

The guests arrive for a distinguished dinner party at the wealthy English estate of Richard Orwell Mortice. But why would he invite so many of his enemies into his home, along with a Scotland Yard Inspector? When the maid discovers good ol' Rick O. Mortice dead, the Inspector and his overly eager Lieutenant sidekick are out to discover the culprit! Everyone has a motive, and the accusations fly— but not before they go ahead and sit down to a luxurious meal. After all, why let one stiff ruin dinner? *(Requires 15 participants. Includes full, reproducible script, invitation templates, nametags, place settings, and a full set of host/hostess directions. Templates available online for free download.)*

Murder at Surly Gates
A Mystery Party Game for Teens and Adults
By S. E. Thomas

Tensions are high when the cantankerous residents of Surly Gates Nursing Home have to put up with money-hungry relatives, a spoiled brat, and her incompetent mother during visitors' hours. When the nursing home manager turns up dead in his office, everyone is a suspect! Who had something to gain from his death? What happened to Badger's heart pills? Why does Lily, a former beauty queen, still try to swing her hips—even behind her walker? Buster, a resident and former security guard, and his son, Doyle, a bumbling cop, want to solve this case! *(Requires 15 participants. Includes full, reproducible script, invitation templates, nametags, place settings, and a full set of host/hostess directions. Templates available online for free download.)*

Accuracy
A Mystery Party Game for Teens and Adults
By S. E. Thomas

A successful, but pompous, author is murdered on the night of his new book debut celebration. A note—intended to stop the murder—actually spurns the killer into action due to some rearranged punctuation. Who wrote the note? Who tampered with the note? Who carried out the false instructions? Nearly everyone has a motive! An intelligent Spanish lawyer with a very thick accent discovers the truth. *(Requires 11 participants. Includes full, reproducible script, invitation templates, nametags, place settings, and a full set of host/hostess directions. Templates available online for free download.)*

Let Them Eat Cake
A Mystery Party Game for Teens or Adults
By S. E. Thomas

A reputable cake contest is underway and the contestants are vying to win 20% of the stock in the wealthy contest sponsor's restaurant business. Then the sponsor turns up dead! He ate an entire cake ridden with arsenic-bearing apple seeds! Who gave him the cake? Who wanted him dead? Why in the world didn't he stop at the first bite? A bumbling security guard who is allergic to flour is on the case! *(Requires 14 participants.)*

A Full-Length Christmas Production for Your Church or Christian School!

A Reason To Celebrate
A Full-Length Christmas Production
By S. E. Thomas

For most, Christmas is a time filled with joy. But for many, Christmas can be a difficult season. Some of us may even feel that Christmas is not a time of celebration, but of sorrow…. But let us consider a moment what Scripture tells us of the first Christmas. What really happened? For the first time, God Himself—the Creator of the Universe, the King of Kings, the Everlasting Father—stepped into our world! He stepped in—not to enjoy the wealth or  the beauty or the joys—but to experience our suffering, our longings, and our sorrows. And, even from the moment of His birth, He experienced far from ideal circumstances. And yet, we remember His words, "In this world you will have trouble. But take heart! I have overcome the world."

Soon to Come!

THE GALAXY TRILOGY
Enter a dystopian future of terror and adventure with…
Book I: Force Down the Night
Book II: The Third Underground
Book III: Sixteen Digits

Acting Out Loud
Christian Skits and Dramatic Readings
By S. E. Thomas

Whether you are a pastor looking for a skit to help really drive home your message, a ministry leader looking for a dramatic reading to speak God's love at a Christian retreat or conference, or a youth group leader wanting to spice up a youth meeting, we have the material you're looking for!

This book offers Biblical skits, skits dealing with issues relating to the Christian walk, evangelistic skits, skits for special events, and holiday skits. Now your audience can experience what it's like to wait their turn in the Hades Complaint Department, learn how to bless others from the Fastest Tongue in The West, or get a glimpse into the hectic life of a pastor through these dramatic presentations that, while fun and entertaining, also deliver a powerful, godly message.

Please Visit Us Again!

Find books, plays, skits, mystery party games, fundraising resources, free downloadable program templates, writers' resources, and much more at:

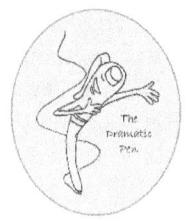

www.thedramaticpen.com

Write To Bless The World

www.ingramcontent.com/pod-product-compliance
Lightning Source LLC
Chambersburg PA
CBHW072150170626
46813CB00004BA/1742